ST. IVO

Joanna Hershon

ST. IVO

FARRAR, STRAUS AND GIROUX
New York

Farrar, Straus and Giroux
120 Broadway, New York 10271

Library of Congress Cataloging-in-Publication Data
Names: Hershon, Joanna, author.
Title: St. Ivo : a novel / Joanna Hershon.
Description: First edition. | New York : Farrar, Straus and Giroux, 2020.
Identifiers: LCCN 2019054818 | ISBN 9780374268145 (hardcover)
Subjects: LCSH: Domestic fiction.
Classification: LCC PS3558.E788 S7 2020 | DDC 813/.54—dc23
LC record available at https://lccn.loc.gov/2019054818

Designed by Richard Oriolo

Our books may be purchased in bulk for promotional, educational, or
business use. Please contact your local bookseller or the Macmillan
Corporate and Premium Sales Department at 1-800-221-7945, extension
5442, or by e-mail at MacmillanSpecialMarkets@macmillan.com.

www.fsgbooks.com
www.twitter.com/fsgbooks • www.facebook.com/fsgbooks

1   2   3   4   5   6   7   8   9   10

For Derek, Wyatt, Noah, and Allegra

ST. IVO

FRIDAY

ESPITE HAVING PUT EXTRA EFFORT INTO drying her hair, into taming her brows, into all the routines that had become more exhausting and more necessary in the recent terrible years, Sarah arrived early to the meeting. Looking around the aggressively charming room, she was overcome with a scrubbed-clean sensation that she couldn't immediately identify. Sarah reminded herself that there was no reason for this surge of positive feeling, that she'd surely have heard something over e-mail or text if there were any real reason for it. But when Caroline arrived in a burst of clashing patterns, with her thick black hair upswept in a jade-green banana clip that looked improbably fashionable, Sarah recognized the feeling; it had been a while: *hope.*

"Oh, honey," Caroline said, with an enviably unrestrained hug. "I can't believe it's been a year."

"I know." Sarah nodded. "I know."

"It always goes so fast, doesn't it?" Caroline sat and whipped out a pair of plum-colored cat-eye reading glasses, quickly scanned the menu, and placed it facedown.

This year, Sarah thought; *nothing fast about it.*

"So," Caroline began, "I don't think you're actually interested in what you sent me."

"I'm not?"

"No. I'm sorry but you're not. That's not where the fire is. *But,*" Caroline said meaningfully.

"There's a but."

"I expect the world of you and always will. You know that?" Sarah nodded dutifully.

"I have a suggestion. Are you open to hearing it?"

"Of course," Sarah said, exasperated. "Of course I am."

The waiter appeared. She became flustered while ordering—"I'll just have what she's having"—as if she needed Caroline to see any more evidence of her inability to think clearly. And of course Caroline insisted on ordering a bottle of Sancerre. Sarah had originally loved Caroline's penchant for daytime drinking, and at the outset it always sounded like a great idea, but Sarah always felt slightly paranoid after sharing a bottle with her, as if she'd spoken too candidly or else had said too little.

"You look so nervous," Caroline said, as the waiter walked away. "You don't need to look like that. Not with me." Her mouth twisted like a little fist before offering a smile more practiced than all the smiles that had ever preceded it.

This lunch, Sarah realized, *might be our last.*

Caroline leaned forward. "I think you should revisit the other script."

Sarah felt a pulsing in her temples. "I told you I couldn't do that."

Caroline nodded. "I know you did."

"When I was working on that script, Caroline—it was as if I had no choice."

"Exactly." Caroline nodded. "*That* is what I'm saying. That's how it read, even then, when it was so raw."

"I still can't believe I showed it to you. It was a mess."

Caroline nodded. "It was."

Sarah shrugged. "Even though it was a mess, I thought that script had a beginning, middle, and end. I didn't realize that the story I was telling—that was just the beginning."

"So, this is what I'm trying to tell you: You have perspective now. You know where it can go."

"I know where it went. But I can't write about it. I'm sorry, but I don't want to. Not with this ending."

When their salads arrived, Sarah made sure to take a few bites. The beets were too vinegary, the greens too spicy; she took several sips of wine.

Caroline shrugged. "You don't need to commit to reality. The story can be whatever you want it to be. And maybe making a film about it—"

The wine suddenly tasted cloying; heat flushed Sarah's arms, her face. She nearly spat it out.

Caroline touched the napkin to her mouth and held it there for a moment.

Then this woman of unshakable nerve, this person who had believed in Sarah when no one else could see her talent, her agent of over twenty years, her one remaining connection to a professional reality, closed her eyes before placing the napkin gently on the table. "I shouldn't have brought it up."

ON THE TRAIN BACK TO BROOKLYN, Sarah bit her nails down to the quick, after a summer of successfully growing them out. Never would she have imagined ending up as someone who rarely wrote more than an occasional fragment, or for whom the shame of not working was so familiar. She tried reminding herself that she still taught a class (Film Aesthetics 1 & 2) each semester at New York Film Academy and she sometimes returned to the screenplay idea she'd sent Caroline, but Sarah knew what working felt like and what it took out of her, and this was not it.

Nearly a decade ago she had promised Caroline a second screenplay. It was the reason for this annual lunch; every year, the Friday after Labor Day, they met to discuss her progress. She hadn't any new screenplay to deliver, but she had sent five pages of notes and ideas about Queen Victoria's daughter Alice, who breastfed her child against her mother's wishes only to have her infant daughter reject her milk and then, after securing a wet nurse, decided to breastfeed the wet nurse's son. Up until Sarah had sent the e-mail, the fragments of this story lived only in a document on her laptop entitled "third project," as if Sarah were so entirely uncommitted to Queen Victoria's forward-thinking and emotionally complicated daughter that she couldn't even bother with a working title. Regardless of how polished or unpolished those pages were, a period film would be too expensive to produce even if she could call in some final favors with her stylist friend or get the wardrobe sponsored. She knew it was a nonstarter and yet somehow she'd sent it anyway.

Sarah had made one film, over twenty-five years ago. It had been lauded as strange and beautiful. She'd made this film quickly and cheaply, never imagining its success and certainly not imagining that it would be the best thing she'd ever do. She'd spent her youth writing stories and had made this one film out of a desire to escape and to conjure, but she couldn't do either anymore.

To use one's imagination for art or even for leisure: this seemed like the world's greatest luxury.

Here was the thing she couldn't get used to: she had only one story now. It was obvious to everyone who knew her.

She closed her eyes and tried to let these thoughts roll by, to shift her focus to something good. She'd felt real and true excitement a couple of months ago, hearing Kiki's voice for the first time in eight years. Her old friend had left a voice message, then e-mailed within the hour. Both times she said she realized it had been years since they'd spoken, but she just had to tell Sarah and Matthew about the new arrival.

We had a baby, Kiki had written. *A girl. I hope I'm not wrong in thinking you'd want to know.*

Sarah had called back. She left her own voice mail, then wrote an e-mail asking for pictures. *Of course of course of course. Of course I want to know. THANK YOU. I'm thrilled for you. And I can't wait to hear everything.*

Kiki wrote back with the weekend invitation. *Make it a long weekend*, she wrote. *Stay till Monday if you can.* She suggested, to Sarah's relief, they dispense with the back-and-forth and just catch up in person. She sent the address and a P.S.

We sold our house in Silver Lake and rented this house, sight unseen, in a town we'd never heard of. Kiki included three overtly tense rectangle-smile emojis, but, knowing Kiki, what she was really saying was *It's an undiscovered gem. You'll see.*

Moving from Los Angeles to upstate New York seemed a particularly strange choice, given Arman's acting career. If it were any other couple, it might have sounded depressing. But because it was Kiki, because it was Kiki and Arman, moving to an unknown town in upstate New York with an infant seemed straight-up glamorous.

None of the four of them—amazingly, Sarah supposed—were on any social media. Matthew had a presence for his company, but that was different. When she searched out Arman and Kiki, Arman was on IMDb, and Sarah had turned up some reviews of a few films he'd been in. Kiki's textile company had a website—which had popped up about five years ago during one of Sarah's semihabitual Google searches. Kiki's designs were made with ink and watercolor, the patterns abstract and lush.

Sarah kept her eyes closed and pictured one of Kiki's underwater-kingdom images. What was she going to get the baby? She'd already made a special trip to a store in Boerum Hill, where she'd become overwhelmed with choices: tiny fleece vest? Exquisite ash-and-maple stacking blocks? The felt crowns and natural-fiber dollies and mobiles made from locally sourced tree branches sent her into a minor panic. It was such a perfectly curated aesthetic of how to raise a person. She hadn't bought or made anything like this for her own daughter. Would any of it have helped? A silly thought—how could it have possibly?—but she did wonder. She questioned everything.

While gripping a Ghanaian beaded gourd-rattle, she'd felt her shoulders tense and her whole self grow suddenly, inexplicably hostile at the sight of perfectly folded onesies in shades of beige, gray, and celery, colors too chic and muted for anyone under thirty. She'd almost taken a cab straight to Target for a more mainstream selection, but if the haute-hippie baby store had so undone her, she shuddered to think how she'd react in this mood to that toxic plastic morass. She'd gone home instead and congratulated herself on having the good sense to take a bath sprinkled with vetiver oil. Afterward, from the comfort of her warm home, which she was unreasonably fortunate to have, she ordered a monogrammed L.L. Bean sail bag in a cheerful Prussian blue, only to realize at checkout that she didn't remember how to properly spell the baby's name, and though she scrolled through her e-mails, she couldn't find any message from Kiki with that information (even though she felt sure she'd received one). E-mailing Kiki to ask how to spell her baby's name would seem somehow inexcusable, as if Sarah hadn't been paying close enough attention.

AND HERE SHE WAS NOW, on a subway with her eyes closed, reliving the boozy lunch with Caroline, wincing yet again at Caroline's suggestion. It occurred to Sarah—not for the first time, not by a long shot—that she'd become a difficult person.

She opened her eyes and opened her book.

Having barely finished a page, she heard:

"I see you are an intellectual."

She continued reading without looking up, offering the same curt smile she reflexively gave to men on the street who said things like *Baby, you looking for me?* Sarah startled easily. It was one of the first things her husband had noticed about her, how uneasy she was. She had never been able to decide if the observation bothered her or if she appreciated it. He'd also liked her hair—long, dark blond, and straight, with blunt bangs— which she basically hadn't changed in thirty years.

"It is unusual," the voice said, "to see someone with a hard-cover book."

She sneaked a glance across the car. He was somewhere between professorial and homeless. He was older— grandfatherly—with a worn tweed coat too warm for an early-September day that still felt like August and a full head of gray hair that hadn't been recently combed. From his accent she guessed that he was Eastern European.

"I'm no intellectual," she said.

He asked what she was reading and Sarah said it was a novel, and when this didn't satisfy him and he asked what it was about, she said it was about baseball.

"You are a sports enthusiast?"

"No." She explained in an irritated rush how she loved books and movies about sports but never the sport itself.

"You're not a *fan?*" he asked, as if the word itself was amusing.

"Never," she found herself saying. "I'm distrustful of teams."

"I understand," he said, which caught her off guard. She smiled.

Why was she chatting like this? She had never spoken to a stranger on a train. Once, on the F, many years before, a Chinese woman had reached into a cloudy glass container, pulled out a hard-boiled egg, and handed it to Sarah's toddler. Sarah was both disgusted and touched and had let her child accept it. She thanked the woman, who didn't speak English, so they'd just smiled at each other periodically for several stops until the woman got off at East Broadway.

"Are you a professor?" the man asked.

"I told you I'm not an intellectual."

"And not all professors are, I am afraid to say."

"Mmn."

"Are you . . . an actress?"

"An *actress?*"

"I'm sorry?"

"Professor to actress? Funny jump. Never mind—I'm neither. How about you? Are you a professor?"

He laughed and then started coughing.

"I'll take that as a no?"

"Are you a doctor?" he countered, his cough petering out.

"I guess I'm a filmmaker." Immediately she wished she'd lied. "Although I haven't made a film in years."

"Ah." He nodded. "And why is that?"

"Not telling."

"I see." He raised his eyebrows; she felt a fresh wave of shame.

The Q train shot across the Manhattan Bridge. Orange-pink light and the old man's face. The sun was far from setting; his jaw was strong beneath sagging skin. As he'd shifted his body to listen to her, there'd been a whiff of something. If he'd been younger, she might have registered this smell as unhealthy and antiseptic, but because he was old, because he was wearing a worn tweed jacket, her brain came up with camphor, moors, a splash of wet wool.

"So," he persisted, "your films; are they documentaries? Sagas?" He smiled.

"No, I made two feature films. The first one I wrote and directed. The second one I was hired to direct."

"How wonderful. And were these films shown in theaters?"

"Yes"—she blushed—"but it was a long time ago."

"This is wonderful," he repeated with such delight it was as if he'd made a bet with someone that very morning that he could find, while riding public transportation, an acclaimed filmmaker.

"My first film did well, actually," she felt compelled to add, though for whose benefit she wasn't sure.

He clasped his hands together and nodded. "This must have been very exciting."

"I guess it was." It was hard not to feel touched by his seemingly genuine interest. "I mean—it was. But I was so young and I really had no idea how unusual it was for a first feature to make a profit, or to get into the good festivals, be reviewed—all of it."

"This film that . . . 'did well'—as you say—what is it about?"

"I just meant in comparison to the other one." It was misguided, she had learned, to assume she couldn't seem arrogant to others just because she held a low opinion of herself. "It's about a young white woman from South Africa under apartheid. She moves to Iceland to work in a fish-processing factory."

He didn't respond and she wondered if he'd heard her.

"I don't know. It was the nineties. It's almost like it happened to someone else. Though my husband shot it—he was the cinematographer—so I know it happened; I mean, he can verify that I was there, that I was . . . in control." She laughed a little anxiously. "Do you ever feel that way about some of your memories?"

"Do I feel as if my life has been determined by another? Do I feel as if someone else has made certain decisions and has— look—taken this action or that one? Yes, of course. But this is a very common feeling, no?"

"Is it?"

"Of course it is." He waved his hand as if to cast away any notion of singularity. "And, this . . . this story—why did you write such a thing?"

"I'm not sure. I've always said it came from seeing a photograph of these women in Iceland removing their snowsuits and revealing chic dresses underneath, around the same time as reading many articles about the Truth and Reconciliation Commission in Cape Town, but to tell you the truth I'm not sure how the idea started. I mean, I know I've seen that photograph, but I think the story might have come first. I met someone at a party who was visiting from Reykjavík." Sarah shrugged.

They were underground again. She caught a glimpse of her reflection in the grimy black of the subway window, with those under-eye circles still new enough to give her pause. "I don't remember whether I met the Icelandic woman or saw that photo first. Anyway, it's not autobiographical—the film—in case you were wondering."

"I wasn't. I do not make stupid assumptions. In addition, you are clearly an American."

"Glad to hear it." She was suddenly grinning and friendly, if also insulted by being *clearly* American. She was teetering on the verge of actual joy simply by talking to someone who knew nothing about her and her constricted little life. "Are you visiting?"

He nodded. "And you?"

"Me? No." It was pleasant to imagine she was visiting New York. That she could pick up and return to another life, her real one. "No, I don't travel much. Although I'm headed out of town for the weekend."

"Somewhere nice?"

"I'm visiting old friends." She suddenly realized that when she had envisioned this visit—walks in the woods, swims in a lake, wine in a spacious kitchen—there was no baby.

"Good friends, I think?"

"She was a good friend." Sarah nodded. "He was, too, in his way. But it's been a long time."

The man shrugged and waved his hand again, as if he were now dismissing the notion of time itself.

"My husband travels so much for work; when he's home, we usually end up staying put. And you? Do you travel a lot?"

"You know," he said, taking his time, "when my wife was alive, she always wanted to go to this place and that place and I did not want to go anyplace. I thought I hated to travel. As it turns out, I enjoy it very much."

"Well, that's great. I mean, I feel kind of bad for your wife, but—"

"Don't," he said sharply.

"What?"

"You needn't feel bad for her."

"Okay. No, I only meant—"

"It is very humorous to me when people use this expression: 'Do you think people ever really change?' Because of course they do."

"I agree," she almost whispered.

"I'm sorry?"

"I said I agree." She cleared her throat. "People change. People definitely change. We tell each other these lies all the time, every day. Like 'You look the same.' *No one looks the same.* We tell ourselves so many lies about time. The way we deal with time. We're all just—hurtling toward death. But it's like—'Oh, people don't change' and 'You look the same' . . ."

Her words shredded the air with their shrillness. She should have kept reading.

The foreign man said, "I am a visitor here. You are a little bit strange and I am grateful for your conversation."

"I am a little bit strange." She settled into a smile. "It's true."

"As am I."

"And where are you from?"

"I live in Washington." As if he'd just remembered. "Washington, D.C."

"And before that?"

"I come from Prague."

"Oh! I love Prague."

"Yes?"

"I've been several times. My husband had a fellowship there a long time ago, soon after Havel was elected. He shot a film. He was a filmmaker, too, I mean, back then," she found herself explaining; was she boasting again? "The crew was Czech."

"I see. It was a good place for foreigners at this time. Our beautiful buildings, our young idealistic people." He smiled archly. "And of course the low cost of filming."

She shook her head. "No—I mean—it was so much more than that."

"Yes?" He looked into her eyes, and for a moment she didn't know quite how to respond. His eyes were bottle green, his eyebrows and stubble stark white.

"It was more than that. Everyone was so knowledgeable and passionate and—"

"You were young. Yes? You were very young."

She laughed uncomfortably. "Well, sure."

He rooted around in his jacket pocket and produced a torn piece of paper. There was a scribbled address, the words *St. Ivo.* "Are you familiar with this restaurant?"

"Here in Brooklyn?" She was disappointed that he didn't want to know what she loved about Prague. "I think so. But I don't think it's a restaurant."

"No? He told me that it was."

"Who did?"

"My son. He is the owner."

"Oh. Well then, I guess it is." She paused, as if he'd caught her in a lie. "I thought it was a bar. I've passed it but I haven't been inside."

"Do you have children?"

"Children? No."

"Ah. I see."

"That's right." She smiled, showing all of her teeth. "It's just my husband and me."

"I see." Then, after a moment: "Is this my stop coming up?"

"You're meeting your son at his restaurant? Then yes."

"You are a filmmaker. I should like to see your films."

"Well"—Sarah tried not to sigh—"as I mentioned, there are two. One is terrible. One might just hold up. They . . . exist." She told him her name. "The first one might have actually been dubbed in Czech."

"I'd prefer to see the original," he replied sternly. "I see plenty of English films, you know. And I read in English quite well."

"I'm sorry," she said, rushing, "your English is excellent."

He rummaged around in his pocket again and took out a small notebook and pen. "Write your name."

She did. "There's only one of me." And when he looked confused: "My name. It makes things easier online."

"Oh, I do not use the Internet." The subway slowed. "Please, write down your address and your telephone number, and this way I may telephone or write to you if I cannot find your films."

That a stranger would ask for her home address so earnestly, without any sense of self-consciousness—it was so old-world, so wildly out of step with their time.

What Sarah suddenly wanted: to be in Prague in spring with her daughter. To sit in the unremarkable café that was remarkably still there each year they'd returned. To order pastry after pastry. To talk about the various museums and castles they'd surely visit the next day, the day after. To listen as her daughter came up with a theme—Mythological Creatures, Death, Kafka—and to sit side by side, *by her side*, playing the same game they'd played while traveling since she was ten years old: you write a sentence and fold the paper over, and the other person writes a sentence, and together, without seeing what the other person has written, the two of you tell a story.

She wrote down her phone number.

The subway doors opened; he was going to miss his stop.

She scribbled her home address.

He grabbed the notebook and looked at her. His green eyes were clear—insistent, even.

"What?" she asked, not exactly uncomfortable.

"You are a good mother."

"But—"

"You are."

Then he disappeared into a rush-hour crowd. Watching him from afar, he looked younger, almost rakish. She felt genuinely stunned and as if someone were watching her.

Maybe she'd misheard him. Maybe he was one of those people who thought women's lives were incomplete without having a child, and—having assumed she was much younger—had said, *You'd be a good mother.*

But his tone, that insistence, had suggested he'd known she was lying. And also suffering.

Kiki had once said something about how Sarah's face invited projection. During one of their first late-night talks, Kiki had declared—in her intimate way, initially so destabilizing—"People must assume they know you."

"Why do you say that?"

"No signifiers. You could be from so many different worlds."

Sarah had laughed, even as she felt judged. "Are you saying I'm—what? Generic? A blank slate? Neutral?"

"I just bet you're familiar to different kinds of people."

Sarah remembered feeling unusually comfortable in that moment with Kiki. It was true. People *did* often think they knew her. And she'd never thought to question why.

This was probably why the Czech man had started speaking to her on the subway. Or he understood she was vulnerable and was somehow trying to con her. He had singled her out, flattered her, and it had worked. She'd told him—a complete stranger—that she was leaving town for the weekend; then she'd written down her home address. Sarah reflexively checked that her wallet was in her bag. She opened her wallet to make sure all the money and cards were there.

She jogged up the station steps, sat on a park bench in the oncoming dusk, and typed *St. Ivo, Brooklyn*, into her phone. She scrolled through Yelp reviews, blog mentions; was she searching for proof that he'd been telling the truth? Verifying that this bar had food service? That someone with a Czech father worked there? And who was St. Ivo? She found, through the oracle of Google, that he was the patron saint of lawyers and a sometime symbol for justice. St. Ivo was also the patron saint of abandoned children.

The cloudless sky thrummed with pearly light, and a text came in from Matthew—*How was seeing Caroline? Where are you?*

Where was she?

She went over the lunch and the subway ride, unwittingly weaving together two sets of images and phrases, until she forced herself to think of anything else, and a group of kids—maybe eight years old—popped into her head. They took Wilderness Skills classes in Prospect Park and she often saw them here, dismissed around this time. The kids were so cute and also easy to mock: Wilderness Skills in Brooklyn! But it wasn't too difficult to imagine how, when autumn came and when the park's entrance became a dark mouth blowing bitter air, the idea of knowing how to use a compass would seem pretty shrewd.

She imagined a son—a boy named Alex—his expression as she approached. He was lanky and freckled, with a mop of dark hair; big feet, dazzling smile. Even though she always picked him up from the park, his face lit up every time.

She supposed she wasn't the only person who daydreamed these glimpses: other children, other husbands, other lives. She dreamed of the children she might have had, if this or that pregnancy had taken, if this or that man had been hers.

Sarah once met a woman in the support group who was significantly older than she, and though the woman looked tired and sad, she also looked stylish. Sarah remembered a blush-colored bouclé sweater and what solace Sarah had taken in the care the woman clearly showed herself. She'd been frank about cutting off her daughter. "I'm done," she'd told Sarah. "It's over. She's not getting any more money. I've already given; do you know what I mean? I gave at the office. I gave at the door."

Where was she? Where was Sarah?

I'm with our daughter again, Matthew. And everyone calls you Matt except for me.

You're making lush short films that no one will see because it's the dawn of the 1990s and there's funding and interest and no Internet for the foreign man on the subway to ignore, and I am with our daughter. I'm sitting on the pine floors of our kitchen in Prospect Heights a million or twenty-four years ago after feeding the baby breakfast, and I'm seeing the grooves in the honey-colored planks, the bits of food that are stuck in those grooves that I need to remove with a special knife kept specifically for this purpose. I'm with our daughter—twelve, thirteen years later—different apartment, different world—as she laughs so hard at the TV that I think something is wrong with her (could something be wrong with her?) and then I start laughing, too, because her laugh is contagious and, yes, just a touch scary, the way the best laughs are.

She rose from the bench and started walking. Maybe she was being followed. She walked faster, developing a stitch in her side. If Matthew had just texted her, it meant he'd finished his long run, which he did most Friday afternoons when he wasn't on a shoot. Despite the side stitch she began jogging toward where he usually finished, suddenly eager—frantic—to see him.

HE WAS STRETCHING HIS CALVES, standing on the curb, lowering one foot at a time. He looked strong in his gray running tank, but when he stopped midstretch and took a swig from his water, ran a hand over his unshaven face, he looked instantly exhausted. Unsettled, she tried to imagine what she'd think if she saw him right then for the first time.

He was looking into the park and didn't see her until she was almost at his side. His face lit up; it did.

"Surprise," she said. She wasn't being followed. She felt both relieved to realize this and also a bit silly.

"What are you doing here?"

"I know it's pathetic, but I always need an excuse to get myself to the park."

"So I'm your excuse?" He put his hand on her neck.

"You are." She gave him a kiss. "Except I'm tired just looking at you." She licked his faint salt taste from her lip. "How many miles this time?"

"Ten." He took another swig of water. She'd bought Matthew his hydration belt—an awkward transaction that should have been conducted online, because when the JackRabbit salesman had used the term *hydration belt* she'd cracked up inappropriately (not an unusual occurrence during that period) and he'd clearly taken offense. She'd bought this gift over a year ago in an attempt toward thoughtfulness, toward acting like the kind of woman to whom Matthew might want to stay married. She hadn't imagined his running habit would stick. This seemed ridiculous now. Equally ridiculous was how she almost *hadn't* bought the hydration belt because she hadn't wanted it to seem as if she were pressuring him to keep up the running. He'd never been in shape. He was the big, tall guy who could get away with never exercising. Between the two of them—and granted this wasn't saying terribly much—she'd always been the athlete.

"Do you feel like Superman?"

He had crow's-feet fanning his eyes when he smiled. He'd always had them, even when he was twenty-two. "I'm creaky."

"Well, I'm impressed." Her gaze wandered inside the park, scanning the meadow, the hill. "I really am."

"Thanks." He twisted to crack his back. He winced before saying, "So tell me about Caroline."

"I will."

Had the Wilderness class come out of the park yet? Had the kids been carrying those orange fishing rods, or compasses, or assorted unwieldy sticks? That's what she wanted to ask. Whether he ran six miles or twenty, it was all the same. Matthew had asked about Caroline. Did he, too, have another, truer question?

"What are you looking for?" he asked.

"What do you mean?"

"You keep looking into the park."

"I don't."

"You were just looking into the park."

"I seriously don't know what you're talking about."

"I'm talking about the fact that you were looking over my shoulder in that direction." He was still smiling. "You're being really cagey."

"Cagey?" She laughed a little. "I'm being *cagey*? What, like I'm actually waiting for someone else? I came here to meet someone who isn't you, even though I knew you'd be right in this very spot?" She laughed, in a forced way, she knew, but it was still laughter. Their arguments were mostly over strange looks, a funny, weird expression that might pass across his face or hers. They could go back and forth about a sideways glance. It was oppressive. And inane.

"Let's stop this," she said.

"I'm stopping."

"Let's go."

"I'm going."

She raised her eyebrows in annoyance but said nothing more. They walked over the stones of Prospect Park West. The streetlights came on early, set for fall, wasting electricity. She pictured the months to come; she hoped for the same changes as always. She pictured phone calls, relief, the smell of burning leaves. This weekend she would say to Kiki, *My phone is an actual appendage*, and Kiki would be ready to commiserate about technology and how it spiritually breaks us down or fucks us up, and then—midsentence—Kiki would realize what Sarah had meant. What it felt like to wait for a phone call; the one that had to come but didn't come.

But.

To be in a car with Matthew on a highway going somewhere in the name of fun. To see Kiki and Arman after so many years. She took Matthew's hand and held on tight. She admonished herself to be grateful. We're reconnecting with friends, she thought, as she took his arm. *Will you please stay focused on this welcome surprise?*

"So," she said, "when are we leaving?"

"Aren't we going tomorrow morning?"

"Well, that's how I left it when I hung up the phone. But Kiki being Kiki said to come whenever."

"What does that even mean?"

"I guess it means we could drive up tonight if we're feeling inspired. She did seem genuinely relaxed about it."

"You always thought Kiki was so relaxed."

"That's because she was."

"Okay, so she was the most relaxed person I'd ever met, you're right. But that was a long time ago. They have a baby now. I'm sure she's not relaxed and I'm sure they need to know when we're coming."

"I can't believe they have a baby."

He didn't say anything.

She silently counted to five.

"After so many years of not having and not wanting one," she continued. "They *really* didn't want a baby. Do you remember? So they changed their minds. I don't know why I'm surprised. It happens, doesn't it? I mean, more often than not, people end up changing their minds."

"I guess."

"What?"

"No, I guess I just assumed it was an accident; they're younger than us, aren't they?"

"They are," Sarah said. "By a few years, they are."

"What's funny?"

"What do you mean?"

"You're grinning."

"Am I?"

"*What?*"

"No, it's just that it hadn't occurred to me that it was an accident."

"Why?"

"I don't know—her tone of voice? That she seems really, crazily happy?"

He nodded vaguely. Sarah felt him disappear. Even though this happened often enough, she was always unprepared.

"Maybe they tried to have a baby for ages. What would we know?" She heard her voice rise and fall, catching on a jag in the center of her throat as if she'd swallowed a pit. "Eight years was a lifetime ago."

THE SUMMER LEDA TURNED FIVE, Matthew found a garden apartment that shared its outdoor space with neighbors because the fence between the yards had been destroyed during a hurricane. Sarah had just finished shooting the second film, the studio film she was hired to direct, which she already knew was terrible. She wasn't in the greatest mood. They signed a year lease without meeting the neighbors, who were away for the month, and hoped they (a) wouldn't be crazy and (b) wouldn't mind that Leda rose at 6:00 a.m., desperate to run outside. Several weeks after Leda had colonized the backyard with her assorted dolls and their accompanying castles and ballet schools and hospitals and movie theaters, the neighbors returned from their trip and introduced themselves that same night with a bottle of limoncello. After learning they'd come from Rome, where Arman had had a small part in his first movie and the two of them had taken the rest of the month to travel, Sarah marveled at how they'd had the energy to be friendly after a transatlantic flight; she would never have managed to be so polite, so social. This was how the friendship took root: Arman and Kiki were always better behaved; they always led the way. When Arman emerged from the apartment, he was usually fresh from a shower and a shave. He remembered to drag Sarah and Matthew's garbage to the curb if they forgot, and Kiki cooked but it didn't even seem that she was cooking. *What are you making? I don't know, I'm just slicing these sweet potatoes really thinly. What will you do with them? I'm not sure.* And they'd be sautéed and served along with exotic greens and cheeses and there'd be bread and wine and Leda would taste everything, eat slowly in a way she rarely did with anyone else. Kiki was a public high school art teacher. Sarah remarked how Kiki's students must adore her. She and Arman both played with Leda—not only patiently but with engagement—and didn't seem to mind the collection of plastic toys inevitably strewn around their cool, childless area of the garden with its mod thrift-store table and chairs and heavy marble ashtray. Sarah had imagined they were interested in having kids one day, but a week into their friendship Kiki offered up her disinterest in motherhood in the same guileless manner that she prepared meals. Sarah found this disarming and felt a surge of affection toward Kiki, a sensation that may have stopped short of sexual attraction but was easily as primal. Sarah could be (she knew) a bit easy-come-easy-go about friends, but she recognized that her feelings were not remotely neutral toward this person. Her immediate attachment to Kiki took her by surprise, but she didn't question that Kiki felt the same way. Maybe because of this deep and unfamiliar certainty,

Sarah finally stopped apologizing for the mess, for not cooking, for Leda's singing at the top of her lungs with tremendous cheer as if she were auditioning for Disney or pretending to be a dog for hours at a time. Sarah stopped insulting her work on the studio film, stopped insisting the only reason her first film had been any good was because Matthew had been the DP. She stopped making self-deprecating remarks about how she'd been pregnant at Sundance when her first film premiered, so each photo of her was a fat photo, and how she'd been no fun. She stopped making dark jokes about how young she'd been when she'd found herself pregnant with Leda.

She started to relax. One night in late summer—or maybe early fall—they let Leda fall asleep under the table while in character—*Good night, doggy*—and she slept for three hours. Everything seemed heightened, their laughter more hysterical, as if Arman, Kiki, and Matthew were all daring Sarah to keep having fun. She knew they should have carried Leda up to bed, but the night was warm and Leda was sleeping, wasn't she? What had they laughed so hard about? Which stories had they told?

SEPTEMBER IN THE CITY was still her favorite time. The hard shine of the afternoon began easing itself into something softer. The sweat of her schlep to the city and back had dried and disappeared. Families were making their way out of the park and toward the subway, the bus; some would go away for the weekend. Matthew ran a hand through the thin, graying hair she was grateful he still had. She wasn't supposed to care about these things—after all they'd weathered, how could she possibly? But she did. She felt a stab of tenderness, but as she began to tell him about Caroline's suggestion that she write a script about it all, she realized, too late, that she should have kept it to herself.

"Have you ever?" Matthew asked.

"Have I ever . . . ?"

"Have you ever thought about making this your next film."

"A film about Leda?"

"Yes, about Leda. About us. Have you ever thought about it? I know you're not into autobiographical material, but I also know you recognize a good story. I know how your mind works."

"Do you?"

"Yeah, I do. And I would not be surprised if you *thought* about writing something. Even if you never intended to make it. You're a filmmaker. I don't care if you never make another film, I will always think of you as one."

"Well, that's dumb." She shrugged, tears brimming. "Or maybe just sad."

Why had she told him? She had no interest in his open-mindedness or his sympathy or disgust at the idea of fictionalizing and likely sensationalizing Leda and their family, or—least of all—what she realized he was working up to right then: how maybe it was worth considering.

"I can't believe you think I should do that," she said. "I really can't."

And just like that, she didn't care about the light or the season or the Wilderness camp or even Matthew. She turned from him and could, in that moment, have walked off forever. She remembered the beginning of their separation. With no daily need to maintain a display of hope, something about being alone had been distinctly *not* sad. With nothing between her body and the sensation of loss, she realized she'd been protecting him from precisely how dark she'd become. She was relieved to be free from that charade, from him.

"I'm not saying that; I'm not. Slow down. I'm just saying—"

"You're *just saying?*"

"I'm just saying. Has it ever occurred to you that it might even help?"

"Help?"

"Yes."

"*Help?* Help with what exactly?"

"Look"—he shook his head—"I don't know. It has crossed my mind that it might help. If you could make a film . . ."

Despite her being too furious to speak, she stared at him, moved by his desperation.

"Forget it."

She nodded.

"I don't understand why you're so upset."

"That's clear."

"It's a suggestion that—" He stopped himself.

"*What?*"

He shook his head and she waited it out. His expression said this was her doing, that she was forcing him to say something they'd both feel uncomfortable hearing out loud. "Look, I'm surprised she hasn't suggested this before now. She's your agent. It's a suggestion. It doesn't mean you have to write the thing."

"I know that. I know *she's my agent.*" She turned toward the trees.

"Where are you going?"

She didn't know. She turned farther into the park. They'd been back together over a year now, and the memories she'd held on to from their two-year separation were overwhelmingly the sad ones, marked with shame and regret. The men she'd encountered—they'd been placed inside the narrowest stairwells and smallest bathrooms and corners of her memory palace at the end of a long dark hallway. It wasn't as if she *never* walked down that hall and peered inside, but doing so had become depressing. But with a spike of righteous indignation, she remembered: it hadn't all been sad.

"Sarah." He raised his voice; she slowed down but didn't stop; he caught up to her side.

"I'm not interested in my own stories. You know that."

"Maybe you should be. Or maybe you should stop pretending you want to make another film. Maybe you should—" He stopped himself, shook his head.

"What?"

"Pivot."

"Pivot?"

"Instead of putting yourself in the position of lying to Caroline every year. Instead of being in a constant state of not doing what you think you're supposed to do."

She surprised herself by not lashing out. "You're right," she said softly. She took a deep, exaggerated breath and slowly let the air out. "I should have taken that foundation job."

"I, too, was a *storyteller*," he said lightly. "Remember that? I won a couple of prizes. I had the grant. I thought I'd be an *auteur.*"

"I thought so, too."

"I pivoted."

"You did." She nodded, bit down on the inside of her mouth. "One of us had to. It's not like either one of us had any reason to think we could actually make films for a living, right? I mean, who gets to do that?"

"I'm not saying I didn't want to pivot, but—"

"You supported us. You're *still supporting us*. You can't have any idea how grateful I am." Her voice sounded raw and too intense. "Also," she added, lightening up, "you happen to like money."

"Everyone likes money."

"Some people like it more than others."

He ran his hands through his hair again and over his face. "It's work."

"I know it is. And you know, Matthew, that I'm not afraid of work."

"I know you think—"

"You don't, actually," she said, low. "You don't know what I think. Why do you suppose Caroline's suggestion bothers me so much?"

WELL OVER A YEAR AGO, Sarah had met Leda at the bottom of the Baja Peninsula, off a bumpy road scattered with horse dung and broken glass. The parking lot had been swarming with flies; giant scorched palms framed a broken gate. Her daughter led her over a muddy path. The ocean roared in the distance.

It's not how I pictured, Sarah had said.

Is it ever?

Leda walked ahead to where the thicket of palms opened up, and when Sarah stood beside her and saw the beach, Sarah gasped. The ocean was cobalt, the sand was white fading into gray as the ocean pulled itself back and back again, revealing the wet sand below. Two wild horses galloped a safe distance away; the two women headed toward a rock outcropping a quarter mile down the beach.

Leda wasn't wearing sunglasses or a hat. Sarah suppressed the urge to mention yet again how Leda would ruin the unlined, unfreckled fair skin that she had inherited from Sarah's side of the family and that would—Sarah promised!—be etched with lines and scattered with liver spots seemingly overnight.

Please, she remembered telling her daughter, amid all this absurd beauty, *please, please, come back*. The wind was making Sarah's eyes water. She fought the urge to shout, *You are killing us*. What she said instead: *I'll find you a job*.

Leda had laughed in one hard peal. *What if I don't want one?*

Sarah willed herself not to react. She said calmly, *I will find you something*.

You will?

What does that mean?

Mom. Leda came close and took hold of her mother's shoulders. They were exactly the same height. *When's the last time you had a job?*

•   •   •

"I'M NOT SAYING YOU'RE AFRAID OF WORK," said her husband now. "What I'm saying—if you actually listen to what I'm saying—"

When? Leda had asked, with her fingers tightly gripping her mother's shoulders.

When Sarah saw Matthew's face go from frustration to what looked like fear, she thought he might be having a cramp in his ribs and silently congratulated herself for not assuming he was having a heart attack. But then she registered the gun in her face, and it was so shocking in its clarity, its heightened crisp quality: metallic, gray, *gunmetal.* They were walking under trees in the park; they would eventually head toward home. The smell of charcoal heating up, potato chips, sunscreen, garbage, urine; the progression toward dinner; even the argument: it was—if not exactly comforting—familiar, pacifying, even boring. She'd turned into the park, asked Matthew a question that was more indictment than question, he had tried to defend himself, and there was the barrel in her line of vision. *Gunmetal.* Used that shade on her toes for years. The gun was in her face; she found it difficult to swallow; a wave rose up inside her and she was going under.

"Jesus," said Matthew. He'd been behind her and now he was grabbing her upper arm, as if she were a child about to run into traffic. "Okay," he told the man in front of them, "okay."

"Gimme your shit," said the man. He wore a ski mask and gloves—must have been sweltering—he wasn't white, not black, not Asian nor Hispanic. He was tall, big; he was a gun. Matthew almost never lost his temper, but she was instantly afraid that in a panic he might go off, punch this man, land them both in further danger.

But he'd already handed over his phone and his watch. "Here," said her husband. "Take it."

"Fuck that," said someone.

"Gimme your bag." Did she detect a speech impediment? Slightly slurred?

"Fuck you."

She hadn't recognized her voice as her own. Her heart was racing fast—faster than the third and last time she tried cocaine, years ago. "No," she cried out, as he waved that gun at her. "I'm not giving you anything." Matthew had handed over all he had. It was Sarah shouting "no," Sarah gripping her bag as the gunman grabbed the skinny strap.

"Gimme the bag."

"Enough," said Matthew. "Jesus, Sarah," yanking her bag.

"*No!*" she yelled, fighting him now, too, both sweat and a chill prickling her skin, egging her on to scream at the top of her lungs, but she didn't scream; she bit down on the insides of her already chewed-up mouth. "No."

"*Give it!*" the stranger shouted.

Matthew successfully tore the bag from her and tried to hand the man everything, but Sarah reached into it, scrambled and failed to grasp her phone.

Then a spike of pain—unprecedented in its shock if not its intensity—pain that sent her off the pavement of the path and onto the damp, cool ground. The man with the gun had shoved her; her face—left side—had hit the pavement. These facts struggled to make themselves clear, to rise to the top of her consciousness and meet with the throttle of pain itself, as she registered heavy treads of rubber soles rushing away. She heard the sneakers through her own high-pitched wheeze on top of coughing; for a moment she struggled to breathe. She saw nothing but staunch gray bark. Undulating green. *I am a big old tree*, she'd sung to her baby daughter, *stuck in the ground is me.* She sat up too quickly and felt blood running down her right arm, which was confusing because her arm felt fine. The blood was coming from her arm? Her eye? Her nose. The blood was coming from her nose. It was gushing from her nose and down her arm.

Matthew came into focus. "Jesus, Sarah," he repeated, keyed up. "Are you okay? Honey?" Taking her face in his hands, looking, checking. "Here"—he took off his running tank—"bleed on this."

"I'm okay," she said, after what felt like a full minute, but still she wasn't sure. "I'm all right, I'm fine." She touched the tank to her nose—there was tingling, throbbing, but most unsettling was the blood.

"Let me see it again," he said, and she moved the tank away.

He gently put his fingers at the bridge of her nose; she flinched but didn't cry.

"I don't think—" she started to say. Two dogs were barking in the distance. Blood wasn't exactly gushing anymore. "I don't think it's broken."

"Jesus. But, yes, I think you're right."

She'd been mugged at gunpoint. Their assailant had shoved her hard, her hands were scraped and stinging, but here she was: still breathing. Her face hurt but not enough that she was worried. She should take an Advil, though. She always kept a bottle in her bag in case of bad cramps, because despite the expectation that her period would begin tapering off—she was almost forty-nine, after all—no such tapering had occurred. As she reached for her bag, she realized that of course the Advil was gone, because her bag was gone and, most important, her phone.

"We have to get some ice on this," Matthew said, and helped her up to start walking.

"It'll be fine." She nodded. "I'd know if something was broken."

When she'd been threatened, her heart had raced. When her face hit the pavement, it amped up more. Now, in the aftermath, she could barely feel her heartbeat at all. She thought to herself, *He won.* This clarity was grounding. Her uncle had been mugged on the Upper West Side in the mid-1970s at knifepoint. His reaction was to look the mugger in the eyes and say, "I know you're scared, man. Here's what I'm proposing: I need enough money to take the train back downtown. I'm giving you everything else. Don't be scared. Okay?" The mugger had nodded, put away the knife, taken all but the subway money, and sent Uncle Dave on his way.

She'd secretly thought she might be that kind of person. But here was proof that she really and truly was not. She was shocked that she'd fought back.

"He didn't know who he was dealing with," Matthew said. "Jesus Christ. He really didn't."

She nodded, annoyed—furious really—at how her vision was blurry with tears. She was fine. There was plenty to weep about, but not this. She recalled the gun so close to her face, how the man in the mask was bigger than Matthew. She'd bitten down on the insides of her mouth hard enough to draw blood there, too; the taste of it was nauseating. "What was I thinking?"

"I mean"—Matthew nodded, he kept nodding and nodding—"Jesus, you really didn't want to quit."

She took a deep breath and then took another. Why did he keep saying *Jesus*?

"*Christ*," he muttered.

"I can't tell"—she heard her voice wavering—"if you're amazed or disgusted."

"Amazed," he answered quickly, standing slightly apart, ready to catch her if she fainted. "I'm definitely amazed." She could tell he wanted her to know he was thinking solicitously— watching her closely, taking extra care. She felt strangely fine other than for her sudden urge to push him over.

In the distance, a group of teenagers walked into the park. A few carried what looked to be lanterns. Was she hallucinating? They were dressed in black and walked in total silence. She noticed two girls holding hands. Their mouths, she realized, were taped closed.

But Matthew was watching them, too. "A protest."

She wanted a bowl of pasta and a big glass of wine. She wanted to climb the nearest tree. She wanted to stick her face in a bag of ice and head straight to Kiki and Arman's. She also wanted to rip the tape off those soft, young mouths. "We have to call the cops, Matthew. We need to file a report."

He nodded quietly.

"You were so calm," she said, before he could say more. "I mean, really. Thank God you were so calm."

SATURDAY

B Y MIDDAY THEY'D CHANGED THE LOCKS. The mugging was already on several neighborhood blogs: a woman was punched in the face before sunset in Prospect Park near Ninth Street after a man demanded her belongings and she refused to hand them over. There was no mention of any other man, any husband.

"It's like you weren't even there," she said, closing the laptop with an unsatisfying click.

"At least you weren't actually punched in the face," Matthew muttered. He'd stayed in bed with her instead of rising early, then brought her a latte and an almond croissant. "Fuck. Just . . ." He trailed off and paced a bit.

She flung her overnight bag on the living room couch, stuffed socks into running shoes. "Do you think I'll want to go running?"

"You never go running."

"Maybe we can run together?"

Matthew sat down on the edge of the deep windowsill overlooking their block, which was visually chaotic. Brownstones and Federals flanked one modern folly across the street with skinny wood slats all along the exterior, a home better suited to a eucalyptus grove. Farther down the block there were doors boarded shut, doors with peeling paint, and glossy painted doors with distinctly modern house numbers—what Matthew called *renovation font*. Their own door was glossy, but as of now their house had no number, and they might possibly move before getting around to choosing one. The block was constantly under construction. During the day, the only reprieve from the buzz saws, jackhammers, and shouting men came during earliest morning and right around dusk. Though buying this house had been their impulsively optimistic move after getting back together, Matthew would have been happy to flip it and buy something else, but they'd only been living there for a year and Sarah wanted to stay long enough to see what it was like without such a racket. The window was open: city air blew fresher than was actually possible; a far-off siren wailed, but aside from that, the street was weirdly quiet. Plus his knuckles cracking, his knee bobbing up and down, the dishwasher's almost imperceptible hum from the open-plan kitchen—she took it all in and ran upstairs for a sweater. Downstairs again, she folded and refolded it and—

"You sure you still want to go?" he asked.

"I want to get out of here."

"Don't you think we should stick around in case—"

"In case what? We have the answering machine for the landline. If the cops really need us, they'll call. I'm fine, and I want to get going."

"I have to tell you," he said from his spot on the windowsill, "you don't really seem fine."

"What's that supposed to mean?"

"I mean, you look *almost* fine—which is strange—I was sure you'd have more bruising and the cut isn't actually that bad, but—"

"You mean I don't seem fine because I'm, what? *Edgy?* I'm edgy, okay? I admit I'm definitely edgy. But I'll feel less edgy in the country." She'd spent a good half hour working with concealer and powder, only to take most of it off. Now she swiped on some mascara without looking in the mirror, blinked several times. "So let's go."

"I just think—"

"Matthew? Let's just go."

·   ·   ·

HE BLASTED DJANGO REINHARDT, drummed on the steering wheel while driving north, annoyingly immersed in the music.

"Do you remember Leda's essay?" she asked suddenly. They hadn't spoken in a good forty minutes.

She knew he hated turning the volume down to listen, especially in a moving car, but today she didn't care. If her injuries and possibly budding PTSD were bad enough that he'd suggested staying in the city, if he'd been solicitous enough to bring her a croissant and latte in bed, shouldn't he try talking to her on the drive? She opened the window. He turned off the AC. She closed it immediately. He turned it back on.

She thought, *We're going to talk the rest of the way if I feel like it; I was basically punched in the fucking face.*

"Do you remember Leda's essay?" she repeated.

He turned the volume down. "Which one?"

"I kept it on the fridge?"

"From when she was little. You mean the one we should have seen as a red flag?"

"It wasn't a red flag," she snapped.

"I know. I know. I was kidding."

Out the window on the highway there was a flash of a blue car glinting in the sun; it looked like a sapphire, like—she remembered—Kiki's engagement ring.

"Please"—she kept her voice low and clear—"please don't read into her childhood and turn everything into something it wasn't. Because it wasn't a red flag."

"I said I was kidding. You know I was."

"Well, you know I hate when you do that, so please just don't."

He nodded.

"It was a perfect essay."

"I know it," he said, and she instantly regretted taking him to task. She needed his levity; she knew she did. So why did she insist on fighting it?

If you had the chance, the fourth-grade teacher had asked, *how would you change the world?*

The essays were posted throughout the classroom on parents' night. Ending world hunger was a popular response. So was more television watching and candy eating for humans under twelve.

It's important to argue for change but it is impossible to bend another's will, wrote nine-year-old Leda. *This must be acknowledged and respected, do you see? BUT . . . If I could REALLY change the world, I would have everyone be happy and cheerful, but not TOO cheerful or happy because then there would be too much of it. Do you see? Everyone needs a conflict.*

Maybe it was a red flag. It was all too possible that it *was* a red flag. What kind of nine-year-old craves conflict? The students had not yet been taught conflict as part of a good story, the teacher had clarified. At least not in those terms. "Where did she get that?" The teacher had laughed admiringly. Matthew and Sarah had laughed right along with Leda's delighted teachers during those elementary school years. Leda dreamed of going to unusual places, not Tanzania or Marrakech but more like Tulsa, Cleveland. She loved to climb as high as she could. She was a beautiful child. Exceptional. She was completely normal. She was affectionate, funny. She had always been too intense.

"What made you think of that?" Matthew asked.

Sarah shrugged. "Who the hell knows." She kept her eyes trained on the pines and weeds of one New York State highway, the pale nothing sky. "I'm disoriented."

Kiki and Arman had both been so good to Leda. How could Sarah have let them go? She knew, of course. It went beyond their move to L.A. three years into sharing that garden (leaving Sarah and Matthew to meet new neighbors, build a fence, then move) and everyone's ambitions and Sarah and Matthew's parenthood and beyond how Sarah wasn't great on the phone. She knew why she'd stopped returning Kiki's calls and then her texts, in the same certain way that she knew she'd cry at some point during the weekend when she looked in Kiki's eyes and saw pity. Arman would be able to mask it, but Kiki was too open: she had a face like a Flemish portrait, a face built to cry.

Sarah had been the one to suggest naming her Leda. "It's just a beautiful name," she'd insisted, a quarter century ago. The name meant "joy" in Greek, but there was also no denying the association with the ancient myth, the poems and paintings from Yeats to Botero dedicated to the kinky seduction: Zeus took the form of a wild swan, seducing the queen of Sparta. Matthew had wanted to avoid such dramatic connotation. He'd argued against marking their daughter with that story—that *rape*. But Sarah had prevailed. It was *interesting*, she'd argued. And swans were *beautiful*. What a dope. She'd told herself countless times that a name could not dictate a life, but it nagged at her. Matthew had wanted to simply name her Joy; it was the least they could have done.

"I can't believe you don't have more bruising," Matthew said again. He seemed to be stuck on this fact.

"I'm sore in weird places. It's like the first time I waited tables."

"And that urgent-care doctor told you that you didn't need an X-ray."

"You were there. That's what he said."

"Are you sure he was a real doctor? He introduced himself as *Eric*."

She felt herself softening; she might have grinned. "He did, didn't he? 'Hey, I'm Eric.'"

"I just would have felt better if—"

"What would make *me* feel better would be to turn off this music."

"Come on." He laughed. "It's the best driving music. Doesn't it make you feel awake?"

"Honestly, when I listen to gypsy-jazz guitar, what I mainly feel is prone to yelling."

"But in a good way, right?"

That earned a real smile from her, even some unforced laughter.

He turned the music off.

Before urgent care, they'd gone to their local precinct. She'd wanted to leave when she realized she'd been to this same precinct for Leda, but Matthew insisted they stay. The policemen and women could not have been nicer. They gave Matthew a T-shirt, as his running tank was soaked with Sarah's blood. They were treated to mug shots of solely young black men: "Is that him? How 'bout that one?" She assured them the man hadn't been black and there was no way she could ever identify the assailant—it happened so fast, he was wearing a mask—but they'd kept it up anyway.

"I'm just so glad you're okay," Matthew said.

Silence spread throughout the car, summoning the quiet of the previous night and the deep clean breathing of Matthew at rest. Her limbs had felt heavy and eventually she must have slept because then she bolted awake with the room still so dark that for one brief moment she didn't know where she was. She relived the smell of the metal and the blood in her mouth and scrambled to find her phone to tell her the time. But, of course, she had no phone. She looked at the clock on Matthew's side: it had been only twenty minutes. This went on for hours—in and out of sleep—until she gave in to being fully conscious, sat upright in their bed that faced the windows, watching the darkness bleed into dawn.

She stood up slowly and carefully out of consideration for Matthew, sure, but mostly she stood slowly and carefully because she had zero desire to speak to or even acknowledge another soul and maybe especially not him. She crept toward the window and stood between the drawn linen shade and the glass. She loved the garden, so pallid right then, save one red cardinal taking flight. How the leaves on the neighbors' massive maple spilled over their fence and swayed in the slight breeze created by that bird. How, beyond the shimmying leaves, a beat-up wicker couch and table were offset by overgrown English laurel. She loved how it looked from this vantage as though theirs was a peaceful life.

In the car heading north, the silence between them became its own kind of noise. "I mean," she started, "just—"

He waited a while before acknowledging that she'd cut herself off before finishing anything close to a sentence. "'Just' . . . ?"

She kept her gaze on the horizon. "What are we going to tell them?"

Matthew changed lanes three times.

"Watch it!" she cried.

"About yesterday?"

She shook her head. "Not about that."

"We'll just tell them," he said quietly. "They're good people."

"I know. But—"

"A friend's a friend." He shrugged. "Even if it's been a long time."

"You have a wider definition of a friend. You make friends all the time."

"Okay"—he smiled—"this is true. But so is what I'm saying."

"You're saying they'll understand. *We* don't understand."

"It'll be fine." He kept his eyes on the road.

THEY DROVE AROUND A LAKE, hugging the pine-tree shoreline. Out the window: shadow play on the open road; no signs of public access to the dark and glittering water. There were only houses and docks, boats and privacy. *Privacy breeds mystery.* Who said that to her? Low and naughty. About their time apart: she didn't want to know. She didn't want to hear from Matthew what he had or hadn't done and with whom, and she'd never tell, even if he asked. But she imagined enumerating her experiences to Kiki late at night, on a deck, while throwing stones in the water below. All of the strangers—they blurred together as if they were merely part of a recurring and disturbing dream in which she was strangely powerful. Why she recalled power was unclear. Her memories were—more often than not—of being more than vaguely uncomfortable.

She hoped Arman and Kiki had one of these houses—a house with access and mystery. She'd dive in the water immediately. Forget about greetings or a bathing suit. Forget holding the baby. She'd get Kiki and Arman to jump in with her. They'd swim and swim and—

"It's not one of these houses."

"What?"

"I was just looking at the map, so don't get your hopes up. They're in town."

"How did you know I was hoping?" This question was rhetorical. Anticipating expectation (and its dark twin, frustration) was one of Matthew's specialties. It was no small part of what made him an in-demand DP and now a successful commercial producer. He was also accommodating. He did his best to make people (and, yes, including her) happy. He said yes with so little resistance, so that when he said no—and with how he said it— you didn't question him. You believed that whatever you wanted was not remotely possible.

"Do you know what?" Sarah asked, as they made their way down another winding road and the lake disappeared in the rearview. "I realized recently that of all the things that I find funny, enraged people rank highest."

"Should depend on who's angry."

"True."

"I have to say, I never find your anger funny."

"Never?"

He shook his head.

"Well, that's probably because I'm so scary."

Here came Matthew's wry half smile, the one Sarah teased him was born in East Texas, where he had lived until he was eleven. His Texan half smile tended to emerge when they were at least two hours outside the city. He claimed this was absurd; but there it was.

THERE WAS A RIVER—or was it a creek?—running under a footbridge that led into town. The houses overlooking the water were built fairly close together, some more ramshackle than others. The drooping telephone wires, the creek and the footbridge, the fat mutt lying in a driveway and a seemingly forgotten ladder overturned on a browning lawn, the leathery skinny woman, smoking and pushing a baby stroller full of groceries—it was all offset by lush ferns, daylilies, old stone walls. It was an enervated aesthetic, a bit of a dump. She liked it.

Arman and Kiki's rental was a white farmhouse with a small barn and a shed on about a quarter of an acre. Matthew parked on the street and they got out of the car; he took both of their bags from the trunk. The sound of a lawn mower was mildly irritating, as was the smell of fertilizer. There'd been a patch of lawn in the Brooklyn garden they'd shared years ago. It had pooled with rain or sometimes had been brown and scraggly, but there was at least one spring day that Sarah remembered when the grass had been green and not too buggy and Leda had stretched out, not caring about soiling a purple dress. She'd pointed up at the laundry lines that remained throughout the neighborhood from the days when no one had dryers.

Suddenly Sarah could hardly stand. Though Kiki and Arman had seen plenty of photos and videos of Leda over the years, they had last seen her in person as an animated eight-year-old who still had some baby teeth. Though perhaps Leda had video-chatted with Kiki a few times on Leda's laptop when she was in ninth or tenth grade, Kiki and Arman had last heard her voice—face-to-face—as a child's voice, not the scratchy, admittedly sexy, sometimes plaintive murmur that had perhaps started as a teenage affectation but had long since become an intractable feature. Just as her hair—the golden cascade of girls' drawings—would always be a part of her, no matter how many times she'd cut it off. And her eyes would remain hazel and feline, which was particularly ironic given how much she hated cats. Kiki and Arman's cat Twyla used to attempt a rub against little Leda's leg, and she'd run inside, begging Kiki or Arman to shoo it away.

Mom, she had yelled, that day on the beach, in the wind, gripping Sarah's shoulders as if she might start shaking her. *You've got to stop crying.*

Sarah leaned on the car for a moment. "I'm okay," she assured Matthew, anticipating his concern. "I just need a second." She looked up at the second floor, where lace curtains were drawn closed.

"Does anything hurt?"

"Oh, you know," she said flippantly, "everything."

"Seriously?"

Her hands stung slightly, right where she'd broken her fall. The shadow beneath her left eye was just now darkening into a bruise and pulsed now and then. She was most aware of the cut on the bridge of her nose. "No, no. Just a little vain."

"Come on. You look fine."

One of her least favorite expressions: *you look fine*. This was undoubtedly adolescent, but she'd rather look wretched. Who's ever comforted by *fine*? *Wrecked* or *stunning*—was that too much to ask? And, okay, to Arman and Kiki she'd appear not only duly battered by time, but also actually battered. Maybe it was better this way; there'd be no pretending. She looked up the driveway's slight incline at the yellow-painted door.

After knocking several times, Sarah started to worry that amid all that had happened in the last twenty-four hours, she and Matthew had somehow messed up the day or the time. They left their bags on the porch and went around to the back of the house, where an overgrown lawn led down to the creek. No one was in either of the two hot-pink Adirondack chairs at the water's edge, nor under the café lights at the outdoor dining table, laden with the detritus of what looked like lunchtime. Across the creek there was a house next to the footbridge. Someone had strung up a faded flag as a makeshift shade over several plastic chairs. Thinking it could be a Confederate flag, she felt immediately ill, but she also realized it could be any flag; the sun had blasted it beyond recognition. She'd become paranoid and on edge long before yesterday; the mugging merely gave her a more concrete reason to be wary beyond the day-to-day national news. The sound of the creek was faint but vaguely wholesome. It was, she realized, a beautiful day.

"Where are they?" she wondered aloud.

Just then, two boys came charging out from behind a stone wall, shooting their bright orange Nerf guns.

Sarah screamed.

Matthew called out, "*Whoa!*"

The boys ran past them—"*Sorry! Sorry!*"—the way only kids can pull off apologizing, exuberance somehow trumping insincerity. A hammock hung between two oak trees. It was the kind she'd seen in Baja—solid fabric, like a big sheet—great for napping. A woman popped up and a man laughed while still lying down.

"Well," the man said, "guess y'all won that round."

The boys collected their Nerf darts and ran back toward the creek, talking.

"Little devils," said the woman.

"They're all right," said the man.

"Oh, crap!" the woman cried, noticing Sarah and Matthew. "I'm so sorry! Was that you?" She awkwardly unfolded herself from the man. She flopped out of the hammock. "I heard those screams and assumed it was our friend. I'm really sorry—we didn't see you! I'm Heather."

"Hi," Matthew said; Sarah might have nodded.

Was the woman a babysitter? She had messy platinum hair, a diamond in her nose; running shorts and an undershirt and the man stretched out in the hammock. "I'm Karim," he said, not getting up. "You okay?"

"I'm fine." Sarah showcased her face with a flourish of her hand. "This was just—a crazy accident."

"Oh—no, I didn't mean—I hadn't noticed that. Sorry, though. What I meant was—you screamed loud!" He was smiling warmly, but also as if he was trying to figure out just how unstable she was. "You came from the city?"

"I'm sorry," Sarah now rushed to say, "but do you know Kiki and Arman?"

"Yeah." Karim laughed. "Yeah, she'll be back. Arman had to go, but she and Sylvie are here."

Arman had to go? Sarah resisted giving in to insecurity so deep it felt akin to vertigo. Maybe they'd forgotten? Maybe Kiki hadn't actually thought that Sarah and Matthew would show?

Matthew introduced himself and Sarah, too.

"Are those your boys?" Matthew asked.

"Yep," Heather answered.

"And Kiki is . . . inside?" Sarah asked.

Heather nodded. "She's putting the baby down."

Sarah pictured Kiki and Sylvie Jane Simonian, eight months old; Sarah could almost smell the room: the sheep's-wool-and-grease scent of lanolin, the talc-smelling blankets, so impossibly soft.

Karim finally roused himself from the hammock and asked Matthew about their Prius, ensuring the kind of conversation Sarah instinctively tuned out. Heather went toward the boys and their possibly escalating argument. Sarah surveyed the messy table and started to gather other people's forks and knives and stack their dirty dishes, grateful to have a familiar task. She could just as easily have imagined lying down in the overgrown grass, but the thought of doing nothing gave her a sense of dread, as if lying down might somehow prevent her from ever getting up again.

She had readied herself for the weekend with Kiki and Arman—prepared for an accounting of the years, for Kiki's eyes welling with new-mother tears. Sarah had tried to steel herself for Matthew's matter-of-fact descriptions, because sharing was Matthew's way. It didn't cost him; he told facts without reliving everything. She couldn't do that, doubted she ever would. She'd been prepared for Arman's reaction: how he'd say the right things but still seem removed. Even his own stories—while articulate and animated—had always sounded as if he were talking about someone other than himself. She'd prepared herself for how this strange quality always reeled her in because she never knew if he was going to seem close or distant. Sarah had prepared herself for all of this.

She hadn't envisioned other people.

Heather returned from the Nerf war down at the creek and took a stack of plates. "Do you have kids?" she asked, as she led the way into the house through a screechy screen door.

"I do. One." If this weren't Kiki's friend, if getting caught were not so likely, Sarah knew she would have lied, just as she had with that man on the train. She would've said no, and she wouldn't have stopped there. She would've added that she'd never wanted them.

"Boy or girl?"

"Girl." Sarah flashed to Leda's pale skin and the scars on her arms.

"You're so lucky."

Inside it was much darker and Chet Baker was playing softly, moody and blue. The kitchen walls were red; the wineglasses green, standing in rows on an open shelf, glinting in the dim light.

"I mean, I know I am, too," Heather continued, testy but quiet. "I know I'm lucky. Sometimes I just get so angry at my kids."

Sarah nodded, setting down the dishes. She felt pressure to stay quiet, not to wake the baby.

"I've never gotten so mad at other people," Heather said, scraping food into the garbage.

"Not even their dad?" Sarah offered quietly.

"Karim's not their dad."

"Oh." Sarah turned on the faucet, waiting for the water to warm. "Well then, what about Karim? He doesn't make you as angry as your kids do?"

"Did you think he was their dad because he's black and my kids are black?"

"Um"—Sarah rinsed the dishes, nervous about offending Kiki's friend—"I guess I thought he was their dad because you seem like you're together, and I don't know, you're young and the kids are young and, I mean, you're lying in a hammock taking care of your kids together."

"Well, he's not."

"I'm sorry for assuming."

Heather shrugged, placed the dishes in the sink. "It's fine."

Sarah took another look at Heather, who was older than Sarah had first presumed. "I'm sorry," she insisted, despite herself. She knew she should stop apologizing.

"Are you okay?"

"Am I okay?"

"Your nose is bleeding."

"Shit." Sarah put her hand to her face.

Heather grabbed a cloth napkin from the counter. "It's clean," she said, handing it over.

Sarah pressed the cloth to her face. It smelled like the inside of a shell: cool, slightly salty. "I'm sorry."

"Don't worry," said Heather, as though Sarah were still apologizing for making assumptions when actually she was apologizing for . . . what, now? Bleeding?

She stepped back outside through the screen door, and Heather followed, back into the light-shot day. "Matthew," Sarah called out toward the car. "Listen," she asked Heather, "I'm just curious—did Kiki mention we were coming?"

"Did she—I mean, I think so."

Matthew and Karim came around the house.

"Matthew, my nose is bleeding. Maybe we should go."

"Wait a second." He rushed toward Sarah, searching her eyes, his fingers gently touching her bruise—checking, checking. "Go?" he asked, obviously trying to gauge whether she was overreacting to the nosebleed or to other people being here, or to something else altogether. It enraged her that he assumed she was overreacting, even as she felt she was.

"I don't feel too great," she explained to whoever might have been listening, but right then they heard the simultaneous cries of a baby and the screechy door and the straightforward excitement of Kiki's "You're here!"

Kiki rushed forward with the baby on her hip, the baby whose screams showed no signs of stopping and of course Sarah wasn't going anywhere. "I'm so sorry," said Kiki, through Sylvie's screams, as she embraced Sarah with one arm and then began to laugh while hugging Matthew. "Oh my God," Kiki cried, cracking up, and as she continued laughing, Sarah reflected on how, if their positions were reversed and it was Sarah with the screaming baby, Sarah's laughter would have been out of embarrassment and discomfort, but Kiki's seemed genuine. Her laughter seemed to acknowledge that her baby's crying was so intense and insistent that it bordered on ridiculous and who were we as human beings if we couldn't acknowledge how such a greeting of utter chaos, especially after so many years, was nothing if not funny?

"She's beautiful," Sarah said, because that's what one said, but in this case it was true: the dark hair swept up in stylish whorls, the clear blue eyes all glassy with tears.

"Thank you." Kiki bounced Sylvie around. "Oh, you cleaned up. *Thank you*—" Kiki called after Heather, who was already back inside the kitchen.

Sarah took up the tablecloth, started to shake it out.

"Stop. Please stop. You just arrived. Please. Just sit with me." Kiki and the crying baby took the hammock, and Sarah pulled over one of the wicker chairs. "What happened with your—"

"Face? It's a long story. I'll tell you later. I'm fine."

"You look gorgeous as ever, you have somehow not aged, but—"

Sarah shook her head. "Stop. I mean, don't worry, no one's been beating me up."

"I was gonna say," Karim quipped, before roping Matthew into helping him with the boys, down by the creek.

The baby still cried and screamed, and when a sudden spell of silence began, Sarah realized Kiki was nursing under a voluminous blue-and-white wrap that brought to mind a prayer shawl.

"So," Kiki said, after Karim and Matthew were out of sight, "you met Karim and Heather."

"I did. And those kids?"

"Heather's kids?"

"*Uh-huh.*"

"What happened?"

"No, nothing."

Kiki started laughing.

"What?" Sarah asked. "What?"

"You're such a misanthrope."

"I'm—excuse me?"

"No, I love that about you. I'm so happy you haven't changed. It always made me feel special because I knew exactly how much you liked me."

Sarah tried not to smile. "So we're just skipping the chit-chat? Is that what you're saying?"

"I am." Kiki nodded. "I'm saying let's skip it."

"Okay, so those kids are hellions," Sarah said with a gust of laughter.

"They are not," Kiki insisted, but she was also laughing, as if maybe Sarah was onto something. "They're cute!"

"And their mother, your friend, she seems prickly."

"Prickly?"

"Nice, maybe. But prickly, yes."

"Well . . . it's a long story and it wasn't my intention to have them while you're here and I'm sorry—but they're staying the night."

"Oh. Well, that's fine. I mean, of course."

"They'll leave tomorrow morning. It was a last-minute thing."

"You don't have to explain. It's your house, and, I mean, it looks like there's room for everyone."

"There is, basically. We'll get a little creative." Kiki shrugged. "Thanks for understanding."

"Of course."

Kiki sat up and stretched her neck, readjusted her position; Sylvie squirmed and went back to feeding.

"I had such a hard time," Sarah found herself saying.

Kiki looked at her, puzzled.

"With nursing. In the beginning."

"I thought you nursed Leda until she was two."

"I did." Sarah shrugged.

These were the kinds of memories she'd never imagined could fade, but they had. So many others had emerged between then and now that were more visceral and so much more important. No matter how Leda screamed and no matter how exhausted Sarah was, Sarah had wanted her close at all times—this was a pleasant, easy recollection, even though at the time she'd felt so desperate, so in love and yet falling apart. Matthew would invite people to stop by for a drink, for coffee in the morning— "Just come by whenever," she'd hear him say before hanging up the phone. "Everyone needs to leave," she'd whisper to Matthew, too soon after the guests' arrival. She'd take Leda into the bedroom and shut the door, her gaze shifting between the ravenous pissed-off baby and her ravaged nipples. She often conjured the soft parts with longing, but it wasn't all soft. It was pie for breakfast, it was up all night; it was *leave us the fuck alone*.

But even all of that—it seemed sweet now. Innocent. She'd been twenty-four years old.

Kiki was twenty years older than that.

Even though, at forty-four, Kiki was technically an older mother, and even though she did have noticeable shadows under her eyes and more freckles and lines, nothing seemed old about Kiki. She was petite, stacked, with skinny arms and legs—the kind of figure that everyone wants in high school and can become dumpling-like with age, but Kiki's extra baby weight and time only served to make her seem younger.

When Sarah had been pregnant, people cited all kinds of great reasons to be a young mother. She'd grown more and more excited as her pregnancy progressed, smiled broadly when complete strangers offered their blessings. She'd been a young mother; young! So full of promise! Had she been more energetic as a new mother than Kiki was right now? Doubtful. Would she get to have more time with her daughter as an adult or get to have grandchildren for longer? She could not consider these questions.

Sarah took in all the different trees, busying her mind with guesses at classification: sycamore, maple, a few white pines. "This is such an immediately relaxing spot. And, you know me, I'm rarely relaxed."

Kiki nodded and laid her head back. "It really is. I'm not sure exactly why. It's certainly not the prettiest."

Sarah didn't protest.

"The week after Sylvie was born, Arman got an HBO show—"

"How great," interrupted Sarah.

"Yeah, it was great. Very exciting. Great part. The show was shooting in New York, and since we'd always talked about moving back, we decided—what the hell—to just go for it, to sell our house and come back East. It all happened really quickly."

"Wow. So here you are."

"Yes. Here we are in this strangely relaxing, not-so-pretty spot." Kiki looked up into the tall tree shading them both.

"So what's the part? What's the show?"

"The show isn't happening."

"Oh." Sarah was careful not to sound too crushed. "I'm sorry. What a bummer."

"Yep." Kiki nodded. "But"—she kissed the top of Sylvie's head—"that's the way the cookie crumbles."

Sarah heard the screen door open and close; she could hear the music in the kitchen had been changed to electronica, the volume turned up. "Do you always have a lot of people around?"

"Do I—?" Kiki interrupted herself, and Sarah could tell she was annoyed. "Yes, I guess I do."

"I mean—"

"It's one night," Kiki said quietly, as the door opened again. "We'll have a good time."

Holding the screen door open with her hip, Heather balanced a platter of cheeses and green olives in one hand, and a bottle of wine and an opener in the other. Sarah leaped up to help, a touch more warmly inclined toward Heather after having criticized her to Kiki. Sarah took the wine and the opener, glad it wasn't a twist top, grateful for something to handle.

After Heather arranged the snacks and darted inside the house again, Kiki made a silent face of excitement—Sylvie had fallen asleep—and Kiki inched herself off the hammock and onto her feet, in what looked like an exaggerated pantomime of trying not to wake a sleeping baby. *I'll be right back*, she mouthed.

Sarah had logged plenty of hours in the middle of the night and in darkened daytime rooms, and even though it had been nearly twenty-five years since that relatively short time in her life, she knew it was too late to be putting a baby down for a nap. Kiki was going inside to tell Heather something, and this was fine but not fine. It didn't feel fine at all.

"Is this her bedtime?" Sarah asked, and Kiki shushed her loudly, shushed her in a way that produced a surge of unwanted anger—fury even—for wasn't it a bit hypocritical to shush her so loudly? And why should they have to be so quiet? Why? When it wasn't even dusk—too early for a bedtime!—and when Sylvie obviously was or wasn't going to wake up but wouldn't be bothered by noise—not so long as she was conked out on breast milk, her mouth still attached to her mother's nipple.

Kiki went in the house, Karim and Matthew continued to play with the boys down by the creek, and amid a small property full of people, Sarah found herself alone at a table now laden with snacks and wine. She heard a faraway screech of tires, a closer swarm of yellow jackets, and became engrossed with encouraging a ladybug to crawl from the tablecloth onto her finger. She hadn't realized Matthew was standing behind her, but she felt his hand on her head and, for whatever reason, she didn't startle; she didn't even flinch. His hand felt immediately calming.

"We should just tell her," Matthew said quietly. "Let's just get it over with."

Sarah nodded. "We'll just get it out of the way."

The already-familiar screen-door screech announced Kiki again, this time without the baby, and Sarah was reminded of how Kiki always carried herself as though late to a music festival—her hips going, her arms swinging—in a bouncy kind of rush.

"So where's the proud papa?" asked Matthew.

"Oh, right—I forgot to mention—he's in the city working. But he'll be back first thing in the morning." Then, upon sensing Matthew's obvious disappointment: "He's really sorry. It was another last-minute thing," Kiki said pointedly, to Sarah. "A film."

"That's great," Matthew insisted.

"Being marginally associated with your husband has been personally fulfilling for us," Sarah said, piercing the cork with the wine opener, twisting and starting to pull. "Do you remember," she asked Matthew, "how we started freaking out when we saw him that first time?"

"In *Reason?*" Kiki asked.

"I wish we had a video of our reaction," Matthew said, nodding. "It was like we'd spotted a unicorn."

"You were *that* surprised he was working?" asked Kiki, her smile slightly fading.

"No," said Sarah, "*no!* It was just this amazing thing after losing touch, to see him like that—and in that kind of role."

"No, I get it," Kiki said. "It just would have been great to hear from you."

Sarah looked out at the creek beyond the stone wall, the empty wine bottles lined up like art or for target practice. She looked at the flag strung up as a shade. "Who lives there?" she asked, filling the silence.

Kiki shrugged. "Some guy."

"Have you met him?" asked Matthew, always doing his best.

"Arman has, briefly. He said he was macho and not too friendly. I guess they spoke once about the telephone wires? We keep different hours. I've never even seen him."

"It's amazing to me how you can live next door to people and never once lay eyes on them, and other people you see constantly, even if you aren't neighbors."

Kiki grinned tightly.

"I'm sorry," Sarah said.

"Why?" asked Kiki.

"I'm sorry I didn't get in touch when we saw Arman in *Reason*. That was a really big deal for him and I'm sorry."

"We're really sorry," Matthew added. Though as far as Sarah was concerned, it would have been great, sure, if Matthew had let Arman know he'd seen him on-screen, but reconnecting all together like this, so many years down the line—for both men this didn't seem particularly notable. Matthew went years without talking to people that Sarah knew he considered close friends. This was about Sarah and Kiki, but really about Sarah because their loss of friendship was her fault. Because they hadn't *lost touch*. Kiki had made an effort.

"Anyway, you're here." Kiki leaned forward. "So? How's our girl? What's she up to? I'm dying to hear everything about her. But I think I need to go slow because I can't even deal with the fact that she's twenty-four. She's *twenty-four*, right?"

"Her birthday was last month," added Matthew. "She—"

"She's twenty-five." Sarah cut him off. She tasted the sting in her mouth where she'd bled the night before.

"What'd you do? Did you celebrate with her?"

"We rented a boat," said Sarah.

Some kind of fog lifted. Some kind of bottom fell out.

She ignored Matthew's foot pressing down on hers. All she saw was Kiki's gray eyes. Soon it would be nighttime. Soon enough she would lie in a strange bed, consumed with anxiety, made worse by the lie she'd just told and the many more she was sure to tell now that the first lie was out there. Soon enough she'd be nothing but a feeble cage for her thundering heart, but for now she was looking into Kiki's eyes, shining with pure interest. "We rented one of those boats downtown. It was a little tacky but great."

"Fun," said Kiki. "Do you have any photos? You must."

"She lost her phone," Matt blurted, racing toward the opportunity to say something true. "I never seem to take photos anymore."

"Both of our phones were stolen," Sarah corrected. "Yesterday, actually."

"Oh *no*." Kiki poured the wine. "That's such a drag."

"We were mugged," Sarah said. "At gunpoint."

"*What?* Yesterday? You were mugged at gunpoint *yesterday?*"

Sarah nodded. "That's how this happened." She gestured to her face, as Matthew shifted in his chair.

"No," Kiki said. "What happened?"

"Well"—Sarah was determined not to be maudlin—"it was just inside the park on Prospect Park West, and it wasn't even dark out. This guy just showed up out of nowhere and pointed a gun in my face."

"That's terrifying," Kiki insisted.

"It is." Sarah nodded. "It was. But I wasn't scared. I was . . . pissed."

Matthew put his hand on her shoulder. She knew this was a gesture of affection—even protection—but it didn't feel that way. It was as if he were doing what little he could to stop her from saying or doing one more reckless thing. Matthew shook his head, smiling, as if this had all been an elaborate gag. "You should have seen her."

"What'd you do?"

"Matthew was so calm. It was amazing. He just handed over everything."

"That's what I would have done," Kiki said.

"How do you know?"

"What?"

"How do you know what you would have done?"

"Well, I don't. You're right. But I have a strong feeling. Like I always knew I'd be a great candidate for bed rest. Then I was put on bed rest with Sylvie for two months."

"And how'd you do?"

"I loved it."

"Did you really?"

"Of course I did. I read. I watched movies. I had friends stop by. I didn't have an illness and I was so grateful for that. I just had to rest."

"I'd hate bed rest," said Sarah.

"How do you know?"

"Ha. You know what's funny? When I saw the gun, my first fear was that Matthew would lose it on the guy. But as it turns out I had no reason to worry." Sarah took a sip of wine.

Kiki said, "You don't know what the person is on, what they're capable of. Matt, you definitely did the right thing."

"No question," said Sarah. "But—"

"*What?*" Matthew stopped her.

"I don't think that gun was real."

"What are you talking about?"

"I don't think the gun was real." Sarah realized this had been nagging at her.

"Why does that even matter?" Matthew began to lose patience. "You think that, in the moment, this would have been worth pointing out?"

"No. I guess not."

"Do you need to go lie down or something? Seriously," said Kiki, "I would probably need to just stay in my bed for a while after something like that. I kind of can't believe you're here."

There were so many noises in this quiet place. Insects and birds trilled; somewhere overhead was the low thud of helicopter blades.

"Sarah?" Kiki asked, reaching across the table for her hand.

Sarah shrugged off Kiki's concern, looking at Matthew, who would not look back. Sarah knew that no matter how bad he felt about how she'd been thrown to the ground, he would still be furious with her for lying about Leda, for putting him in the position of having to lie, too.

"I probably am still shaken up . . . You know what I really want to do?" Sarah said, forcefully brightening. "I want to get in that creek."

Kiki scrunched up her face. "I haven't seen anyone in it. It's so close to town and it just looks a little iffy, y'know?"

"There must be a good swimming hole around here," Matthew said.

"You'd think. We've basically spent most of the last month trying to find one. But the checkout girl at the supermarket told me yesterday that *Friday the 13th* was filmed at a nearby lake, so, you know, there's that."

"And the checkout girl was telling you this in order to . . . generally freak you out?"

"Of course. She was giggling with her friend as I left."

"I'll bet it's a pretty good spot," Matthew said. "Right? At least worth a shot?"

"I was getting there. I thought we'd go tomorrow. That's my big plan. Maybe before Sylvie's nap? Or after, if you want to sleep in. If you *can* sleep in. She's a bit of a screamer. I may have mentioned that in the e-mail?"

"I'll just get my feet wet for now," Sarah conceded, heading toward the creek.

She left them sitting at the table. The path to the creek was uneven and weedy and she had to focus on her footing. Standing at the water's edge, she knew she was still close to the house, but it felt miles away. She took off her sandals and stepped in the water, shuddering from the initial cold. If she could shut out her surroundings—the footbridge, the not-so-picturesque beginnings of town, the faded flag that she was starting to suspect was indeed Confederate, and the empty bottles and plastic furniture across the way—if she could shut it all out, she knew the water would feel clean and lovely.

I knew you'd appreciate this spot, Leda had said on that deserted beach in Baja, where sand created a stream of shallow water refilled by high tide. Her daughter jumped over the stream and shouted nonsense to the empty beach.

Are you going to do cartwheels? Sarah had asked. Leda had spent several summers as a child obsessively cartwheeling and demanding an audience for each one.

Shut up, her daughter had said, her smile bright. The sunlight hit her directly in the eyes; she didn't even shield them.

Sarah would probably always wonder if the rest of the trip might have gone differently if she hadn't been sarcastic about the cartwheels. It was absurd, she knew it was, but what would have happened if she hadn't pointed out—no matter how gently—how Leda always needed an audience? Because who cared if she needed an audience? Sarah was and would always be desperate to be in it.

She bent down now and chose a stone from the water. She watched it fade, as it dried, from dark brown to tan. She checked back to where Matthew sat with Kiki at the table. They were busy talking intently. She realized that, from where they sat, they probably couldn't even see her. She turned back to the creek and lobbed the stone as far as she could.

Maybe he was telling Kiki the truth. Maybe that's even what Sarah wanted, and why she'd insisted on walking away. She watched as they rose and started to clear the table. She wondered if Matthew was attracted to Kiki now, though she remembered him agreeing when they first met that she was pretty but not his type. She had pressed him, flirty. *Am I your type?* How could he not be seduced by a woman in the throes of that new-baby love?

Soon the lights would be turned on and the bugs would come out. Dinner needed preparing. She knew she should get up and help them, but she didn't. Nor did she sit in one of those jaunty pink chairs. She stood in one spot with her feet in the creek. She watched the empty bottles and bleached-out flag and how no one there seemed to be home. The greens were turning black, the lavenders gray. By now Sarah's feet were freezing and she began to shiver. She turned around and checked on the house. The lights came on in the kitchen. There was the sound of chatting, laughter. No one came for her. She wished Kiki's friends would go home right this second, that she could close her eyes again and hear their car drive away. Then again, she also wasn't sure what she'd say once she had the chance to be alone with Kiki. It had taken about a year before she'd said anything of significance at her support group. That was over five years ago. It had seemed so weird to reveal intimate details to strangers, most of whom were emotionally wrecked themselves, but life had a funny way of reversing itself, and now she couldn't imagine talking to anyone outside of that room of people—Matthew included—about the details and the questions that continued to haunt her.

A pale woman in a turquoise sweatshirt stopped on the footbridge and made a phone call. Sarah heard nothing but "Fine"—loud, exasperated—before the woman continued into town. Sarah looked back toward the house again. Like a beacon, the outdoor lights switched on. She half expected a flash sequence, a message from Matthew: *Get yourself back; get back.* When they *did* flash, she was so startled she had to catch her breath, even though she knew it had to have been a wobbly circuit.

"I was just about to go get you," said Matthew, as Sarah walked into the kitchen, where preparations for dinner were well underway. The two boys were playing some kind of game that involved yelling and eating Pirate's Booty. Kiki was chopping tomatoes and onions. She looked up at Sarah with tears streaming from her bloodshot eyes.

"Let me take over for you!" Sarah insisted.

"No, it's fine." Kiki wiped her nose on the back of her hand.

"You're weeping! She's weeping!"

Kiki backed away from the onions, as if surrendering. "Why do I insist on doing things that I am clearly not meant to do? Will someone please explain this to me?"

"Drama queen." Sarah smiled, taking the knife from her. "Maybe you're punishing yourself?" She picked up the task where Kiki had left off.

"No, I don't think so." Kiki opened a beer. "I'm too selfish for that."

"You're the least selfish friend I ever had," Sarah said matter-of-factly, not pausing the chopping, but when Kiki didn't reply, Sarah stopped to glance up. Kiki looked surprised—presumably by Sarah's intensity—but Sarah was ill-equipped, somehow, to make light of anything just then. "I mean it."

Kiki placed the beer on the counter. Her face looked inscrutable.

Heather and Karim came into the kitchen freshly showered. She was wearing no other makeup but her lips were bright red. Her hair dripped all over the countertop as she began to count hot dogs. Karim offered Heather a beer and she shook her head. Before opening his own, he put the cold bottle against the back of her neck and she squealed, laughing a touch too hard. Then she held up the hot dogs and, with bizarre urgency, asked the room at large, "Do you think the boys will each have two?"

"Sarah," asked Kiki, "do you want to go see your room?"

Did Kiki realize how annoying her friend was? Or had Matthew told Kiki everything when they were alone outside at that table and, now that Kiki knew that Sarah had lied, was having a hard time focusing on anything while Sarah was in the room?

"It's fine," said Sarah. "I can finish this."

"Look down," said Karim. "I'd say you're finished. Are you a sous chef or something?"

The onion was already diced and her eyes were now tearing, too. "No," said Sarah, suddenly self-conscious, as if she were actually crying. "Just hungry."

"Have a carrot." Kiki pointed to a small yellow bowl, with the tone one might use with a toddler. Kiki began sautéing the onions and garlic, and within a second of those fresh tomatoes and herbs hitting the pan, Sarah went from hungry to ravenous. Though Heather had laid out that platter earlier, Sarah had been too unsettled to taste anything and realized she hadn't eaten since morning, which felt like a year ago. Why had she been in such a rush to get here? Sarah crunched on carrots as

Kiki explained where Sarah and Matthew would be sleeping. Then Sarah walked toward the stairs, passing the two boys, who were finally quiet and lounging on the couch, bathed in the glow of an iPad.

The upstairs landing had bookshelves and, in between the bookshelves, a mini-daybed below a picture window. It was the kind of spot she'd always loosely dreamed of having if she ever owned a house in the country. When she looked out the window, she was met with only her reflection. She thought of the subway and the Czech man and St. Ivo. *You are a good mother*, he'd said. She knew she'd never tell anyone about that moment. It was too strange and it was all hers. She also somehow knew that shabby formal man would contact her. It filled her with calm. She followed Kiki's instructions to their room for the night but passed it by, continuing on down the darkened hall to the master bedroom. She sat in the dark on the unmade bed beside the heap of a rumpled duvet. She caught Kiki's scent— bergamot, lemons, woodsmoke—made out the shapes of small bottles and books sitting by Kiki's side of the bed. Arman's side was tidy, with a stack of papers and a pair of headphones. She thought she heard the baby.

Across the hall, the door was open. She opened it farther, slowly. It was cooler in there with the fan going, and soothing, with a small machine emanating patterned light and the sound of heavy rain. There was no other light, no monitor. The baby lay silent on her back in a zip-up sleep sack, her arms flung above her head as if she'd landed in slow motion right there in the poppy fields of sleep. The sour milky smell was almost sweet, and the appropriately stark crib had no adorable and potentially hazardous pillows or blankets, no plush lambs or bears. The baby's dark hair curled in little wisps. Her lips were pursed as if she'd stopped sucking just a moment ago.

As if Sarah were watching herself, as if her hunger had risen and shown its true focus and relentless velocity, she witnessed how she reached down into the crib and picked up the sleeping baby. She held Sylvie in her arms, and as her little body squirmed just the slightest bit, Sarah whispered the solid stream of *shush*, the hum and kisses until Sylvie snuggled and relaxed, let her softest cheek rest on Sarah's cheek. The feeling was so extraordinary and instantly familiar. It was as if all of her life had temporarily been siphoned away into this one creature's breath. Sarah focused on the muffled sounds of all the people in the kitchen, the clatter of a meal coming together. She stood with the baby by the window. The leaves brushed the glass. Beyond the curtain, the moon: halfway to full, a bone-bluish white. Same same same.

three

SATURDAY EVENING

S ARAH LOWERED SYLVIE—SLOWLY, SLOWLY—into the crib, aware of her still-warm cheek—the left one, where Sylvie's had rested. Every movement, right down to the rhythm of Sarah's shallow breath, felt exposed, criminal. As soon as Sylvie made contact with the mattress, she began to wail. Sarah closed the door behind her before anyone could see she'd been inside. No one was in the hallway. Feathery shadows traversed the walls. She darted down the hallway just as Kiki climbed the last of the stairs; she must have taken them two at a time.

"She's crying," Sarah said, with every intention of seeming relaxed, but it came out strangely grave.

"Yep," Kiki said, passing her by. "I heard her on the monitor."

Had Sarah, while she was in the baby's tranquil room, said anything out loud? She hadn't seen the monitor. Had her desperation transmitted into the kitchen as Matthew and Kiki and Kiki's friends discussed her odd behavior?

Had she spoken?

She remembered only the sweetness of that cheek. How much time had elapsed?

Kiki disappeared into the baby's room, and Sarah just stood there, frozen at the top of the stairs, facing the wall of books.

I know where the books want to go, said Leda. They'd moved into their third apartment as a family. Matthew unpacked in the living room. *Daddy, let me,* she said. *I know where they'll be happy. Boring books can live on the bottom. It's safer.*

Sarah sat—not downstairs joining in, not in the cozy reading nook beneath the picture window, but on the cool, hard staircase. It was possible that Matthew was stirring or chopping in the kitchen, but he could go either way on being helpful during a group meal.

I swear, he'd finally exploded, a couple of months ago. *I swear I haven't heard from her. What's wrong with you that you think I wouldn't tell you? Would you keep something like that from me?*

Would she? She didn't know.

He was in the kitchen now, downstairs, doing what he did so easily: charming strangers into friends. She appreciated this about him; she appreciated knowing him so well.

They were still married.

Once they'd been strangers, Sarah and Matthew. They had been young and entirely separate. She liked to remember this. Also that he'd been in the engineering program, that his parents wouldn't help him pay for school, that they'd wanted him to go to community college. After several weeks of watching him make strange choices in Acting 101 mostly involving silence, she found herself walking alongside him one day after class. By the time they reached their bikes, both locked up outside the same building at the end of the block, she'd learned that he'd enrolled in the class because his grades had dipped because he never participated in seminar discussions, so he'd summoned the courage to see a therapist at the student health center about his crippling shyness about public speaking, and the therapist had decided what Matthew needed was a semester of acting.

You don't seem shy, Sarah had said.

Nice, he said. *I guess it's working.*

Then he'd kissed her. That shy stranger. The wind picked up. She was twenty; he was twenty-one.

They sat in the shade of an oak tree in Madison, Wisconsin. It was a little too cold to be sitting outside. She was wearing a Victorian-style lace shirt. Ripped jeans. Brown oxfords. She didn't remember dates and anniversaries; it was weather and clothing for her. Matthew in a blue flannel shirt. Flannel stretched over a pair of broad shoulders still generally carried erotic promise for her. Unoriginal? You bet. But there it was:

flannel. Blue. Wind. A stick scraping through dirt. Patches of unmowed grass. He cracked all of his knuckles. He cracked his back.

SHE HEARD A DOOR OPENING. She was never in the right place. She should have been downstairs helping already. Instead of hurrying to the kitchen right then, she took a book off the shelf and pretended to be deeply interested in Jewish Buddhists. Kiki passed her on the stairwell, giving the thumbs-up that Sylvie had gone back to sleep. Sarah mirrored her gesture and followed Kiki downstairs. She'd been wrong about Matthew. He wasn't talking to anyone; he wasn't even drinking beer. Karim and Heather were in a heated discussion, but Matthew was focused on a design magazine, sipping red wine. He had a nearly full bottle in front of him. Sarah took a glass from the open shelf. They were both, she noticed, instantly making themselves comfortable here. He didn't look up.

"Why do *you* get to say whether someone's gender identity is real or not?" Heather erupted. "How are you so confident?" She turned to Kiki. "How is he so freaking sure about this?"

"Well," said Kiki, raising one thin eyebrow, "you know."

Heather nodded, gave a shrug. "It's the Karim show."

Karim laughed. "What the fuck does that mean?"

"Shh," hissed Heather, nodding toward the kids across the room. "It means, you know, *Karim decides.*"

He was shaking his head, laughing. "Please." He stopped laughing. "We all decide. Some folks just decide some crazier shit. No *he* no *she* but *they*? They is going to the store? Really, now? They *is*?"

"They *are*," said Heather. "They are. Are. It's a plural conjugation. We've gone over this."

"Do you even know anyone who's gender nonbinary? Either of you?"

"That's not the point," said Heather.

"Who's to say who anyone else is?" Sarah found herself saying out loud.

"Right?" said Heather, sizing Sarah up with what felt like newfound respect.

"I mean," Sarah continued, "I can be really judgmental, trust me, but if a person has the wherewithal to decide who they are and what they want to be called, well, have at it and, I mean— congratulations. You know who you are? Seriously? Godspeed."

Karim laughed. Even though Sarah agreed with Heather, she liked him better.

Karim and Heather moved on to discussing when they should get the boys off the iPad, and just how much, exactly, exposure to technology did or didn't shape a child's personality, which had essentially the same effect on Sarah as a conversation about cars. She wondered if Kiki was as engaged as she appeared.

Sarah leaned over to Matthew and whispered, "I'm sorry."

Matthew nodded.

Then he went from sulkily drinking and flipping through the magazine to making a convincing show of being helpful. Before Sarah could bring herself to start chopping the remaining pile of herbs, Matthew had filled a pot with water. The banter of Karim, Heather, and Kiki grew indistinct, buzzing, as suddenly all that mattered was getting Matthew to look at her. She needed further acknowledgment from him, she wasn't exactly sure why, but without it she felt unmoored. She was trying to be patient, but when she couldn't hold back anymore, she mouthed, *I'M SORRY*, the words overenunciated with an aggressive display of eye contact.

The stove's pilot light had gone out and Karim had been unsuccessful in relighting it, and now Heather was trying and failing, and—while clearly not French—crying out, "*Merde*," as if fulfilling Sarah's unspoken request for just one more example of what constitutes an annoying person. When Matthew took over, he used his Zippo lighter, the one he still carried though he'd quit smoking years ago.

"That's great that Sylvie fell asleep again so quickly," Sarah offered stiffly to Kiki.

Kiki nodded vaguely. Sarah remembered her friend as effortlessly efficient in the kitchen, but now she only alternated between sipping beer and working through an elaborate knot in her hair. Although this may have been nothing more than evidence of a new mother's fatigue, it was easy enough to imagine that Kiki's discernibly slower rhythm was an attempt to stall while deciding how to handle having heard Sarah over the baby monitor. That she knew Sarah had gone into her daughter's room, picked her up, cuddled her until she cried, and snuck out of the room like a failed kidnapper.

"Sylvie's perfect," Sarah blurted out, laughing for good measure. As if self-awareness could somehow counteract such obvious naked longing.

Kiki smiled—was she blushing?—and gave a modest thanks.

"Those little lips and all that dark hair," Heather chimed in. "Forgive me, but my ovaries are pulsing."

"All right, all right," said Karim. "Let's go then." He grabbed her waist.

"He wants a baby."

"I think we got that," said Sarah.

"I've always wondered about that expression," Kiki said. "About ovaries. Does that actually happen?"

It was impossible to tell whether Kiki was mocking Heather or asking a frank question.

"I don't actually ovulate, you know, naturally," Kiki said. "So I don't know."

"Oh," said Heather, "I didn't mean to—"

"I never have. Or at least no one seems to think I ever have." Kiki shrugged and started grating Parmesan cheese. "I'm just grateful to the entire field of reproductive medicine."

"It is incredible what they can do these days," Sarah said quickly, sounding glib and idiotic. Could her sentiments be any lazier? "So Sylvie was—"

"Very much planned; donor egg. Arman's sperm. IVF."

"Sounds like," Matthew ventured, "you may have answered that question more times than you might have liked."

"It's okay. I don't mind people's curiosity. Most people just ask if she was an accident."

"I mind," Sarah said.

"What's that?" Heather asked.

"*I* mind people's curiosity. I'm sorry."

"I remember," said Kiki.

"What?"

"I remember how you hated when people nosed around, fished for some kind of story about why you had a baby so young."

"Only in New York. Elsewhere I was nothing special."

"How old were you?" asked Heather.

"When I had my daughter? Twenty-four."

"What's her name?"

"Well, you also looked younger than twenty-four," said Matthew. "You were usually carded at bars. That added to it."

"I guess I did look really young. I remember feeling ancient."

"A baby will do that to you," said Kiki.

Sarah found herself unable to bear Kiki's being even slightly negative. "But—"

"But what?"

"You just look so young. You really do." Though Sarah was ready to lie about so many other things, she somehow needed Kiki to understand this was true.

Kiki waved her off in a way that reminded Sarah of the man on the subway, how he'd dismissed the relevance of time.

"I just never know," Kiki persisted, "when people use that expression, like you just did—about their ovaries pulsing—if it's real. Seriously. Is it just, you know, a dramatic turn of phrase? Or can you actually *feel your ovaries?*"

"I'm out." Karim laughed again; they all ignored him.

"Well, yeah," Heather said. "I mean, sometimes."

"You can actually feel them in your body?" Kiki was starting to sound—though Sarah could have been imagining it—confrontational.

"You can," Sarah acknowledged. "I mean, I have."

"Well, I can't. But who knows? I could still be a late bloomer. Can you imagine? *And, defying all odds, local woman begins ovulating at age fifty.*"

"I wouldn't put it past you," Sarah said.

Heather started taking the plates and napkins outside; Karim went to start up the grill.

"I'll bring the glasses," Sarah called. "Do we need knives?"

No one answered. But then Matthew and Sarah were finally left alone with Kiki, and Sarah wasn't about to move.

Matthew said, "Kiki—"

"I just didn't want kids until I did, you know?"

Matthew poured himself more wine.

"I didn't know," Sarah said. "About your ovaries."

Kiki was sort of laughing, but clearly nothing was funny. "Come on. How would you have? Even I didn't know until I tried to get pregnant."

"I know, but—I'm sorry. I can still be sorry. That you had to go through any of that."

"I did feel furious at basic biology for so long. I was supposed to have a kid before I was remotely interested in having one, just because I might want one someday. Almost everyone I talked to said I would regret not having done it. I knew plenty of women making the decision to do it even though they were ambivalent, but it seemed like an awfully big one to make, based on maybe, you know, *possibly* changing my mind. And Arman was so focused on his career; I guess he was hesitant, too, but it was mostly me. So we were careful. And then one day I didn't get my period and instead of being worried, I was crazily excited at the thought that I could be pregnant. I wasn't, of course, but the desire *to be pregnant*—it came on so strong I couldn't see straight. I became consumed with regret and obsessed with having a baby *just like everyone said I would*, which honestly made it so much worse when I couldn't."

Sarah felt a jolting pang of homesickness for her family's old apartment, the one where they'd moved just before Leda started middle school. The living room was painted the palest gray; Sarah must have tried ten different shades.

"Did you ever consider not having her? Leda, that is," Kiki corrected, reddening. "You know what I mean."

"You mean did I think about getting an abortion when I was twenty-three? Yes. I did." Sarah didn't look at Matthew. It had been so long since she'd thought about any of this; Kiki had never before asked, so Sarah felt she should answer honestly, in the spirit of their friendship. "Matthew was still Catholic then."

"And I loved her," he said. "And she loved me. There was that part, too."

"There was." Sarah nodded, chastened, smiling at him.

She could see a thought pass across Matthew's face. It settled over his deep-set dark eyes and olive skin, full lips, and reddish stubble. She pictured that pale gray wall in their old apartment at the end of an ordinary day; how quickly a shadow can consume the brightest room. She dug her fingernail into the rough wooden table. The windows reflected rich colors all around them. No Benjamin Moore Calm here. No Dew, Solitude, or Dawn. The water was boiling and Kiki put in the pasta, gave the sauce a stir.

"Was it hard on you?" Sarah asked. "Trying to get pregnant?"

Kiki tasted the sauce and took her time swallowing; she sloshed beer back and forth in the bottle. "Yeah."

This was as far as the conversation would go. Kiki was up for talking about her ovaries and her deep ambivalence about motherhood and how many years earlier (it was a different life for Kiki, too, Sarah reminded herself) she hadn't wanted any part of it, but she clearly had no interest in talking about what followed. What changes of heart and mysterious forces led her to this moment: listening to a baby monitor in upstate New York with two people she used to know well and who now might as well have been strangers.

Kiki's current friends were outside. It seemed more and more likely that she'd asked them to stay so as not to be alone with Sarah and Matthew. Kiki might not have originally invited them to spend the night, but—especially with Arman in the city—she'd wanted a buffer.

"Well, she's here. Your baby." Matthew raised his glass. "And you got a girl. Lucky you."

"Lucky me." Kiki nodded with a smile so radiant Sarah was surprised there weren't tears.

Out the window Sarah saw a flash of fire. She caught her breath before realizing it was only the charcoal grill.

WHEN THE KIDS had finished eating and were set up with a movie, and the outside table was cleared and reset, and when a bottle of rosé was poured and two more plunged into a tub of ice, Karim raised his glass. "To Kiki."

"Hear hear," Sarah said.

"And to meeting Sarah and Matt," Karim said, his glass now in their direction. "You have such good taste in friends," he said to Kiki. "Here's to, *you know, you know*—bringing us all together." Karim put his other arm around Kiki with a playful squeeze.

Across the creek a light started flashing. At first Sarah thought it was some kind of tasteless decoration, but it was inconsistent, like someone with a flashlight goofing around.

"You really don't know who lives there?" Heather asked.

"Nope," Kiki said. "Just a guy. *Some guy.*" Karim and Heather smiled along with Kiki at what was obviously an inside joke. "I've spent so much of my time here indoors with Sylvie. There's the hot sun and the napping and, I don't know, life. Anyway, I get the feeling he isn't my type of person."

Heather grabbed the flashlight at the side of the grill. "Snob." She flashed the light twice in quick succession.

"Right, I'm a snob. You got me. The privilege. My privilege. Go ahead."

"I'm teasing," Heather said. "Jeez."

Sarah felt a reflexive jolt of panic at the notion of this conversation. That she had made her first film at all—that she'd had the audacity to think she could—and then how she'd thrown her good fortune away, all the while being supported by Matthew . . . she knew Kiki must have been thinking the same thing: if anyone here was guilty of inequitable privilege, it was definitely Sarah.

The light across the way flashed three times.

"I wonder what he looks like," said Heather.

"Of course you do," said Kiki, and Karim laughed.

"This is really good," said Matthew, taking second helpings of the pasta and slightly burned vegetables; Sarah wondered if he was uncomfortable or barely paying attention.

Heather flashed the light four times, then put the light beneath her face and gave a maniacal laugh.

"You are not going to get to know our neighbor, Heather," Kiki said. "Not gonna happen." She was smiling but there was obviously plenty of history here.

"Please?" asked Heather, as the light across the way flashed five times. "Sarah, you do it." Heather passed the light across the table.

Sarah shook her head, but then, not wanting to be too dour, flashed the light once.

"Go on." Heather laughed.

Sarah wasn't sure whom she was reacting to when she flashed it twice more, then just lost count and kept on flashing.

"Are you seven years old?" Heather laughed. "He's going to come over here now."

"You told me to!" cried Sarah. She was trying her best to be fun, though she felt pretty strained.

"I'm really not up for this." Kiki closed her eyes and took an audible breath. "Can we just have a calm meal?"

Sarah set the flashlight down. "I'm sorry."

"Sorry, honey," said Heather.

"Some of us just really don't want to meet our neighbors right now," muttered Kiki. "Once you all leave, who do you think will have to actually interact with him and deal with the consequences?"

"I know," said Heather. "I'm stopping."

"I'm sorry," said Sarah. "That was stupid."

It was hard to tell exactly how bothered Kiki was, and Sarah realized she was leaning forward in her chair toward her as Matthew was leaning back. He looked suddenly distracted or indifferent to this exchange, and she was never quite prepared for when he exempted himself from a conversation. Sometimes it seemed as though he lost interest in a moment just as she became fascinated.

Sarah noticed a diamond speck embedded, fetchingly, in the flat cartilage of Heather's ear. "So what about you two?" she asked Heather and Karim. "How did you meet? Why do I have a feeling it's a juicy story?"

Matthew shifted in his chair, obviously disapproving of Sarah's prying, which was infuriating, given how Heather carried herself as if she were practically begging to spill secrets.

"I cheated," Heather said, instantly proving Sarah correct. "I mean, with Karim. He was my friend and I fell in love with him." She took his hand.

Everyone kept quiet.

Sarah nodded, momentarily thrilled to invest in someone else's highs and lows, be they petty or monumental. Why hadn't she understood earlier today how preferable it would be to focus on other people?

"It was messy," Heather said. "But it worked out."

For now, Sarah did not say.

Heather gave a crooked smile. "I knew I'd be resentful if I

kept shutting myself down. I never thought I wanted to be married to anyone besides my ex. But it was . . . so much bigger."

"I do wish you hadn't lied to him at first," Kiki said.

"I know." Heather nodded. "But—" She cut herself off, as if she knew whatever she'd intended to say would be indefensible to Kiki.

"Though you told me you thought he already knew," Kiki said almost pleadingly, and Sarah realized Kiki had been a friend of this ex, maybe still was. "Don't you remember that? Right after he found out? You said you thought he'd known but was maybe okay with it?"

"He didn't know." Heather finished her wine. "I was lying then."

"Oh," said Kiki. Sarah saw Kiki's face change along with Karim's. His easygoing manner was suddenly and completely gone. "Oh."

"If I'm honest"—Heather's voice was free from any nuances that might be construed as even vaguely apologetic—"I think most people stay together out of fear. Most people would be happier if everyone met someone new every seven years or so. And if everyone *knew* they could find someone great every seven years or so, everyone would do it."

"That's bullshit," said Matthew.

Sarah took a sharp intake of breath; she was surprised to hear him speak up.

"Yeah, I mean, it's obviously not a popular position," Heather said.

"I just don't think it's true." Matthew's voice was quiet and direct. "People might go outside their marriage because it's exciting, but they also do it to keep themselves separate." He put down his fork. He didn't drink. "That's fear. Or, you know, maybe in your case, true love." He shrugged. "You'll see, right?"

"How long have you been married?" Heather asked, with no small amount of aggression. "Your daughter is an adult, right? You've been together most of your lives?"

"We separated for a couple of years," Sarah found herself saying. "Recently."

"You did?" Kiki looked so obviously crestfallen that Sarah wanted to say she was joking.

"Yeah," said Matthew, "but it was a good thing, our separation. It was good."

"Really?" Sarah said, before she could stop herself. She felt her face break into a terrible mocking smile.

"Yes. But I don't really feel the need to dwell on that story right now." Matthew looked around the table. She didn't know where his gaze was going to land. She felt the hair on the back of her neck stand up as if the table were on fire, as if Matthew were telling a ghost story around that fire. Then she realized that he *was* telling a ghost story, and that their story was a ghost story; only the ghost changed with each telling. Sometimes Leda was the ghost but not always.

THE KITCHEN DIDN'T have a dishwasher and the sound of the faucet running was comforting. By the time Heather and Karim disappeared upstairs with the kids and the dishes sat on the drying rack, the larger bowls resting on towels, Kiki had fallen asleep on the couch. Matthew and Sarah stood behind her, watching how she clutched a pillow, how she'd curled herself into a ball.

"Did you tell her the truth?" Sarah whispered.

He didn't answer immediately, and she didn't press him.

Finally, he shook his head. "I wanted to."

Sarah picked up a cream-colored mohair blanket and shook it out before smoothing it carefully over Kiki. Then Sarah followed Matthew upstairs.

He kept quiet, and she had no interest in talking—not about why she'd smiled that terrible smile and publicly questioned whether their separation had been a good idea, and certainly not why she'd told Kiki such a ridiculous and important lie. Matthew stretched out in bed, under several thin blankets, and either fell asleep or pretended to. She used to sometimes resent that he'd drop off so quickly at night, but these days she could barely remember that petty impulse. She was genuinely happy for him if he could get a good rest and had grown protective of his sleep. Because she couldn't. The insomnia had improved in the past several months, but the mugging might have cemented her struggle. Her first bout had been in college, but after graduation, while living in downtown Manhattan—the best place to be an insomniac—she stopped worrying so much about it. Because after a few weeks of writing in the same restaurant in the middle of the night, she realized she enjoyed being awake and productive during those hours, and this recognition allowed her to plan a life for herself. Now, when she thought about her youth—her brief true youth—she thought of diligence, rice pudding, blue pen on colored index cards. She imagined bright lights in a bustling restaurant from midnight to 4:00 a.m. Being surrounded by some people eating breakfast, some lunch, and some dinner simultaneously and how this disorganization of people's internal clocks filled her with a sense of tremendous freedom.

The floorboards creaked as she made her way to the bathroom in the hallway, which was pink tiled and too bright, and she kept her eyes down, avoiding the mirror as she washed her hands. When she went to dry them, her thumb brushed against something large and caught in the hanging white towel. The something fluttered so wildly she'd thought it was a bird or a bat, but she swallowed her shriek as she realized it was the biggest moth she'd ever seen, glistening black and fiercely batting the air while going nowhere. Wings beating, light shining, heart pounding—she fell back into the hallway and raced down the stairs.

In the living room, Kiki had burrowed herself under the blanket, and her sleeping mass formed a sculpture moving ever so slightly with breath. One large window revealed only darkness, the outdoor string of lights was switched off, and it was as if Sarah were waiting for the neighbor to flash his (probably drunken) signals again. Or she was waiting for someone to thread the reel, to project images of daytime, any day would do. Or maybe she was waiting for the day to begin. The screening would skip back several hours or days or even years, or all the way back to the first night in the garden with Kiki and Arman, with Leda's toys underfoot.

She sat down next to Kiki.

What did she remember from this time in her life, when Leda was Sylvie's age? A low-level hum of anticipation. It had ushered her through that first freezing winter and helped her push a stroller so fast and far that she never once remembered feeling cold. She looked up: snow-heavy branches; she looked down and the baby's still-blue eyes peeked out from the depths of the stroller.

With the lightest touch, she placed a hand on Kiki's foot; she imagined it would help her feel more grounded. Instead, she felt a light-headed rush, as she realized this was an empty heap of blanket. Kiki must have gone upstairs.

OUTSIDE WITH LEDA that winter there'd been quiet electricity. Her film (*her film!*) was coming out in theaters in New York and Los Angeles the following fall. This had not seemed possible, but she was too consumed with feeding and changing and snuggling Leda to linger on any one thought for too long. For the first time since college her insomnia had vanished; she could barely stay awake at night. What did she see in those moments before sleep? Not her daughter's eyes, or her slow-blooming smile as she lighted with seeming disbelief on her first falling snow. Not Matthew, walking through the door smelling of beer, with a bounty of bagels and M&M's from craft services, courtesy of whatever film he was shooting for next to nothing. Not the reviews that would or would not run when her film came out, or what their life could look like in the wake of success or failure or different choices. Every time she fell asleep she always saw the clock at 2:00 a.m.; she saw her colored index cards and her blue rollerball pens bright in artificial light. In her fantasies she was alone and focused.

Sarah crawled under the blanket. She felt she was crawling into Kiki's skin. She was cradling Sylvie; she was setting a table;

she was walking with buoyancy no matter her age or mood. Only when she heard tires over gravel and saw a flash of headlights did she realize she'd been asleep.

An engine cut out. She awaited the car door closing and the footsteps approaching, and—with somnambulistic logic—knew she had to get up, it was time to get up, and she forcefully threw off the blanket. She was suddenly overcome with claustrophobic heat, and without even realizing she was doing so, she opened the screen door and went outside.

It was humid and cool. Crickets and the sound of faraway cars rolled over the faint ripple of the creek. With only the town's streetlamps on in the distance, the view seemed dingier and more ominous. As she stood at the side of the house, she collected herself by counting her breaths, peering around toward the front, anticipating a stranger.

Arman. Sitting in the car. His shock of blue-black hair.

She didn't approach, didn't wave from where she was standing.

A mild fall evening in their garden, after Leda had gone to sleep. Arman had been more subdued than usual, and when she'd asked if he was all right, he'd reported that an agent who'd initially pursued him and with whom he'd met several times had officially declined to represent him after coming right out and explaining that, though he admired Arman's talent and range, his look was limiting. When Arman had pressed the agent to elaborate, because Arman was no rube and had simply wanted the agent to feel uncomfortable, he'd been told that there were only so many terrorist and cabdriver roles and the agency already represented an actor of that type. Arman was a third-generation

Armenian American from a leafy Detroit suburb. *People have no imagination*; on this they all agreed. *People don't see.*

He was every man, now, alone inside his parked car in the middle of the night, vaguely illuminated by a phone. When he finally did get out of the car, it was with one movement and he was headed in her direction. She hurried away—why?— sinking into the hammock as quietly as she could. It was darker under the trees, and the hammock's cotton was slightly damp. She watched him sit down at the outdoor table; he leaned forward and rested his head on his arms.

She rose from the hammock and realized that no matter how she did it—at this point, in this spot and hour—she was going to alarm him. She figured calling out from farther away would be less frightening. "Hi, Arman."

"Fuck—" He whipped his head around. "What the—?"

"I'm sorry, I'm sorry—" She started to laugh.

"Wait"—he was whispering now—"*Sarah?*"

He started laughing, too, as he rose from the table to give her a hug. He smelled like clean sheets and something stronger, like the funk of the soybean farm where she'd worked during the summer after her freshman year in college. "What the—?" He held her out in front of him in a fatherly way that felt silly and surprisingly sweet.

"*What?*" He was still holding on. "Why are you laughing at me?"

"I'm not, I'm not. You *did* know we were coming, right?"

"Of course I did." He let go of her arms. "I just didn't expect to find you awake, outside, at five a.m."

Now he squinted slightly. He leaned in to touch her face and she flinched.

"What happened?"

"Long story."

"Oh, I bet."

"What is that supposed to mean?" She smiled. Such a tender instinct, to touch her face—tender and startling.

"Did the baby wake you?"

She shook her head. "I *bet*? What does that mean, Arman?"

"Your face is banged up. That's usually complicated, isn't it?"

"I suppose."

"Hey," he said, quieter now. "You okay?"

She nodded.

"Plus"—he smiled—"you're complicated."

"You haven't seen me in years—"

"Doesn't matter—"

"And already I'm complicated?" She could still feel the slight touch of his fingers on her face and tried not to blame herself for that. He'd barely touched her—had it even been a full second before she'd flinched?—but she could feel the lingering warmth, the slight callus.

He shrugged, laughing. "I'm teasing you."

"Yes, well, I was mugged at gunpoint."

"No shit?"

"Absolutely no shit."

"Oh, man, I'm so sorry."

"Yeah. Well, that's what happened." She sat down at the table. "Yesterday."

"Damn." Whereas someone else might have become more

alarmed and animated upon hearing this news, this dose of reality seemed to settle him down. He shook his head as he yawned. "Was Matt with you?"

Sarah nodded.

"Well, that's a relief, at least."

"Is it?"

His laugh sounded more like chastisement. "Hey, do you want a drink?"

Sarah shook her head.

"Mind if I get one?"

"Nope." Even if the sun would start rising in about an hour, it felt like the dead of night. She watched him stretch as he headed into the house. The way he moved—you could tell he was an actor, or maybe a martial artist; he had that self-conscious muscularity. He was rangy and stocky at once. She thought of that restaurant, open 24-7 with its scramble of meals and schedules. She faced the creek and the neighbor's flag but imagined Arman opening the fridge.

"I'm sorry I said you were complicated," he said, coming back to the table with a bottle of beer.

"It's fine. I am."

"I am, too." He sat beside her, not too close and not too far.

"I know."

"Okay."

"Okay?"

"Yeah, okay. I hear you." He yawned his way into a smile. "We're all—y'know—really fucking complicated."

Arman looked older in a way that betrayed a lot of late nights. She hadn't expected that. Though maybe it was cultivated? The beard was a nice touch, especially with the hair on his head still so thick and short. Had he grown the beard for a role?

"Long shoot?"

He nodded.

"How'd it go?"

"It went well, thanks." He sounded strangely polite.

By the time he'd finished a few swigs of beer, she could tell he was unhappy about something. She hoped the source of his unhappiness was particular and not a more general midlife malaise, for which she had little patience. She was about to ask him about it—his unhappiness—but then reconsidered.

He stayed quiet in a way that felt awfully loud.

"Do you want to tell me something?"

He looked at her but said nothing.

She tamped down the urge to ask what was wrong, to be too greedy for information.

He cocked his head, appraising her. "There's always been something a little clueless about you."

"Clueless?"

"Yes."

"Clueless."

"Yes. As in, not having a clue. Being conveniently surprised. Maybe I should say purposefully clueless. I should probably stop talking but—what the hell—I'm not going to." He took another swig of beer. "I wasn't on any film set."

"Okay." She envisioned the nodding and listening faces of her support group.

"Okay?"

"Arman."

"What?"

Out with it is what she wanted to say, but she was trying to be—or at least trying to appear—patient. "Okay," she said instead.

"You don't want to know why I lied?"

She looked at him and felt such a surge of affection that she thought, *I should get up. I should get up and move away.* "Of course I want to know."

"I'm being stupid," he muttered. "I'll tell you later."

"Suit yourself," she said lightly, trying to keep true disappointment out of her voice. Was he cheating on Kiki? If she thought this, why was she acting so nice to him?

"Maybe when the sun is out. Maybe when I've had some sleep." He continued to drink his beer; they both looked out toward the creek.

"You can though," she said. "Tell me, I mean."

He continued to nod and suddenly it seemed as if he might cry.

"You can tell me whatever it is."

"Sarah." He shook his head. "My neighbor! I'm happy to see you."

"I'm happy to see you, too. Let's go inside."

"Nah, I'm staying up." He glanced at his phone. "The baby will be awake soon."

"She's perfect, by the way." Sarah glanced at the sky, still dark. "Just beautiful."

"I know." He smiled. "I can't believe it."

Sarah's smile turned into a yawn. "I'm sorry—" She yawned again. "I couldn't sleep earlier, but now"—she turned toward the house—"I'm just so tired."

"Wait—how's Leda?"

"Leda?" she asked, strangely breezy.

"Yeah, Leda."

She shook her head.

"Well, she's young," he said. "Right? She's young."

Sarah gripped the door handle, turning it, but still not going inside.

She pictured the back of Leda's head, the way her hair went from straight to curly in only one fist-size patch at the back the first time she stopped using. After Leda was released from the gorgeous and expensive rehab facility, they'd lived together for two months in a nearby one-bedroom rental. Matthew came and went, depending on his travel schedule. Sarah and Leda went hiking every morning at the crack of dawn, ate the same salad with blue cheese and pears at the same café for lunch. They went to a hair salon in Scottsdale and asked for chin-length haircuts. They'd laughed their way through an afternoon, through a harmless impulsive decision.

Leda said, *The last couple years have been horrible, haven't they?*

Leda said, *I have put you through hell.*

Sarah fiddled with sugar packets, keys, the newly blunt ends of her hair.

Leda said, *I'm so sorry, Mom.*

Sarah reached for Leda's hand, the edge of her sweater, her face.

We'll look back on this time as transformative, Sarah said. *We'll come to understand just how much we've learned.*

The morning after the haircut Leda was gone and so was Sarah's cash and favorite pair of emerald studs.

"Congratulations, Arman. I haven't said that yet, have I?"

"No, you haven't."

"Congratulations. You're a father."

"It still just feels . . ."

"Unreal?"

"Yeah."

"It'll probably feel like that for a very long time." The rusted metal handle of the screen door was growing warm in her hand. She finally gave it a push.

SUNDAY AFTERNOON

S HE WAS ALONE IN AN OVERPRICED, MOLD-infested Mexican hotel. Her stomach flipped. It was all arranged; she was going north. Her chest and back were soaking wet. She sat up, sneezing, and realized with dead certainty that she was not in Mexico. She wasn't seeing Leda. There was heat, yes, but it was the inland heat of an

East Coast farmhouse bedroom. She tentatively touched the bridge of her nose. It felt as if raising her eyebrows might cause the wound to open and bleed. When she closed her eyes, she saw the gun, the creek, the baby; Arman in the car.

The mild clatter and raised voices coming from the kitchen suggested morning had come and gone. By the time she made it downstairs, no one was there besides Matthew. She went to kiss him, but he looked off to the side while he returned the kiss, as if he were on to the next thing. She had a flash of both of them naked, right there in the empty kitchen.

"I have directions to the horror-movie lake." He pointed out the coffee, with more than a touch of impatience. "Let's go. Let's get in the water."

She slathered a baguette with butter. "Is everyone already there?"

"Karim, Heather, and her kids are already on their way back to the city."

"Thank God."

"What was so wrong with them?"

"Nothing." Sarah headed out of the kitchen and up the stairs again to change. She called out, "I can still be happy they're gone."

"IT'S FUNNY," he said, turning the key in the ignition.

"What is?"

"You seem hell-bent on not wanting other people around, other conversation, nothing obstructing time with Kiki, but . . . why? I'd think you'd be grateful for the distraction." He gripped the steering wheel more tightly. "You lied to her right out of the gate."

"You know I'm sorry."

He rolled down all the windows. "And because I didn't contradict you—how could I?—I'm a liar, too."

"You're not a liar. Can we please turn on the air-conditioning?"

"How about we have some actual weather?"

Sarah kept quiet and found she didn't mind how her sweaty thighs stuck to the car seat. She might as well try to get as hot and sticky as possible so she could enjoy the swim that much more. Matthew had—yet again—turned on the gypsy jazz, in spite (*because?*) of yesterday's conversation, and she kept quiet about that, too, tapping out the manic beat as loudly as she could. Sun shone through pines and maples; they bumped along a dirt road.

"I heard you saw Arman."

She nodded. "It was weird."

"How so?"

"I don't know, I couldn't sleep, I was outside, it was the middle of the night."

"He seems good."

"I don't know," Sarah said.

"Not everyone is miserable."

"Who said anyone is?"

"Not everyone is."

"I'm not miserable."

"I didn't say you were. I said—"

"I'm not."

"I'm glad to hear it."

When Leda was about two, she would begin a crying jag and Sarah would say, *Sweetie, why are you crying?* And Leda would say, *I'm crying*, and Sarah would again ask why and Leda would repeat, *I'M CRYING*.

Sarah put her bare feet up on the dashboard. "It's a sunny, funny day."

Matthew cracked a smile.

"Neither of us got shot two nights ago."

"True," he said. "I like your attitude."

"I'm sorry I lied. I am. I'm really sorry. I just couldn't handle it. But I can now." She stuck her hand out the car window.

"Careful," he warned.

"I'm going to tell them."

"That'll be interesting."

With her fingers stretched apart, she felt the wind pass through. "It will."

THEY EMERGED FROM THE WOODS behind Kiki and Arman's Honda onto a spit of sand. It looked like a makeshift parking lot, and some piled-up charred logs were also off to the side—someone's forgotten campfire. The Honda was idling; they were still inside. Kiki was sitting in the back seat next to Sylvie. Had Sarah done that with Leda? Sat in the back next to the car seat? It seemed a little much. But she must have. They'd rarely driven in the city. She remembered driving with Leda as a baby while taking that first trip to L.A.—the film premiere, her leaky boobs, drinking dirty martinis. She'd carefully pumped her milk and poured it out, watched it circle the drain and disappear, several stories above Sunset. They'd driven on location with Matthew when Leda was a toddler, and later—when she no longer needed a car seat—while on vacations. All of Sarah's car memories involved straining her neck. *Just use the mirror,* Matthew had told her, knowing she'd complain later on, but she always had to go and yank herself around, either to watch Leda sleeping, to hand her a snack, to look her in the eye while making an important point. But did she sit beside Leda when she was a newborn? She must have. Right? Of course she must have. Or else she hadn't. And for all she knew that could have been the missing piece.

"Right, *what?*" Matthew asked, as he cut the engine.

She looked at him blankly, not realizing she'd spoken.

"Right, what?" he repeated. They were both looking at the lake, more impressive than she'd pictured—a matte blue-green.

"Did I sit next to Leda in the car when she was a baby?"

He shrugged.

"I mean, I must have."

"I don't remember." He didn't say it was useless to wonder, but he was obviously thinking it. "I just want you to consider something," he tentatively began. "She's alive."

"As far as we know," countered Sarah, but she was nodding.

"You saw her alive on a beautiful beach just over a year ago."

Sarah looked out the window. As she registered a parked truck with a man sitting on the edge of the flatbed, she had a burst of vigilant energy. Oddly, the man was facing their cars and not the lake. His legs were swinging. She sensed his threatening presence as she riffled through her memories, trying to come up with some tangible proof that she'd sat in the back seat with her own baby.

"'The anguish of death . . . ,'" Matthew said. "We can't—"

"I know," said Sarah firmly. "I know. 'The anguish of death is different from the awareness of self-destruction.' We read the same book."

She reached out and rubbed his neck, made a sincere attempt at softening her tone. This coincided with a wave of what they referred to as beach exhaustion (Sarah's overwhelming urge, upon arriving at any body of water, to fall asleep in the car). But she forced herself to snap out of it. As Matthew got out, she made sure she did, too. The truck, she noticed, featured a Confederate bumper sticker, and so—assuming the flag across the creek from Kiki and Arman's was Confederate—she'd seen not one but two Confederate flags in the span of a day, right here in New York State.

The man was now standing on the ground, facing the water, leaning on the truck and yelling, presumably at the woman in the water. It was hard to tell if he was angry or happy. He was white, stocky. She might as well have been on public transportation: she had the urban dual instinct of acceptance and avoidance. Her eyes went toward the only other vehicle there: a banged-up compact car, the color of dried blood, which had the look of having been parked on this lakeshore through several seasons. The car's decrepitude was sufficiently distracting so she only then noticed the man was not just yelling but also drinking.

"Nursing," said Arman, getting out of his car. "She'll just be a second." Or that's what it sounded like. Sarah had to strain to hear.

"Woman," the man yelled. Then he laughed and tossed

something in the water or maybe at her? She was laughing, too, right? She was laughing.

This man wore boots and pants too heavy for the weather and a tight black T-shirt. The woman floated on her back and closed her eyes, before moving toward shore and sitting in the sand, half-immersed in water once again.

He said, "I told you, you're doing it wrong."

"I am not," she yelled. "Tell him," she called out to them.

"Like they're going to," he said.

"I'm doing good," she insisted.

"Come on, now. One, two, three."

She dove underwater and thrashed around. Sarah realized the woman didn't know how to swim.

The man said, "Come on now. Bitch, you're not even trying."

Kiki and Sylvie were still in the car. Sarah had the urge to knock on Kiki's window and make the sign for wrapping it up. But Sarah hated nothing more than being rushed, and she'd hated it even more when she'd been nursing.

"You're not doing it right," the man yelled.

She was laughing again, the woman in the sand, but now, although Sarah realized she was probably projecting, the woman seemed nervous.

A trail went through the woods surrounding the lake. As soon as Kiki and Sylvie emerged from the car, they'd all get going. They'd walk until the cars and yelling man were nothing but specks in the distance.

Matthew was at Sarah's side. "Maybe we should go somewhere else?" he whispered.

"It's pretty here. Arman," she called, "I'll scope out a spot." And then, low, to Matthew: "By the time we find another place to swim, it'll be time for the baby to go back to sleep."

"Sarah," Matthew said.

"You know I'm right." She started off. "Just help them with the stuff?"

The man in the truck was doing some whooping. He seemed to be imitating the woman. The trail started just beyond the grim parked car. She grabbed her bag and their towels and quickly headed off.

On the trail the temperature dropped. She rolled her neck and worked out the kinks, walked with her arms straight over her head. She realized how much the heat had contributed to her agitation and also how much she loved being alone. She loosely calculated that she needed at least four hours of being completely by herself every day to feel vaguely okay, and she wondered, as she often did, why she wanted so badly to stay married.

When Leda had left their home in Brooklyn for the last time, four years ago, she'd been sober a year and was going on her first solo trip. She never returned. Sarah and Matthew hired the same private investigator they'd hired the first time she'd disappeared, not long after she stopped going to classes the spring of her senior year in high school. Before the PI finally turned up something six months later, Sarah had pushed Matthew away in every sense. She entirely stopped wanting to have sex. She'd become so depressed that she couldn't bear to be around another person, especially a person who was Leda's father and functioning properly in the world despite his private sorrow—when she so clearly wasn't.

Then, just under a year into Leda's disappearance, Sarah had told her husband she couldn't bear to look at him. She'd said he wasn't a man anymore, that she was no longer a woman. She said she was disembodied and he was nothing to her but a reminder of Leda, and she couldn't think about Leda anymore, not for another second. She'd said many things, some terrible, some stupid, all mostly true.

I opened the door a crack and he ran right out is how she'd described it to the support group. They were living separately by then. He'd told her that she had to at least *try* to learn to live with uncertainty, if she wanted to live with him. *Not even you can control this one*, he'd said.

What exactly are you saying? she yelled.

I'm saying you're controlling.

I'm controlling?

Yes.

I see. You mean I'm so controlling that our daughter couldn't take it anymore?

She could still see those specific, compassionate, unsurprised faces from the support group that evening, nodding with recognition. Sometimes—for some kind of warped fun—she imagined confessions that might come close to shocking them.

But then the PI turned up an empowerment retreat through which Leda had booked discount transportation.

Sarah called Matthew in the middle of the night until he answered in a muffled panic. She told him about what the PI had found and begged him to come with her. Then she suggested they fly together, out to Pasadena.

She had begged, but she'd only had to beg once.

Leda was finally sober, but she was also lost to them, and Sarah's job—an important job, according to Leda—was to let her be lost. Since then, there had been moments like this one in the woods on a path—while walking and getting a whiff of something overwhelmingly *itself* such as dogs and their piss in the park, or turpentine from the foundry below the support group's meeting space, or Matthew's neck, or this pine and fir and deep fresh water—when she believed this so-called job to be a valid possibility. In these rare moments when Sarah was shocked out of her head and back into her body, she believed that letting her daughter go was not only what Leda wanted from her, but that she needed to acquiesce; it was maybe the right thing not only for Leda but for herself.

But most of life was nothing like these moments. And despite hearing Matthew say, *She's gone, but she's not dead,* more times than she could stand, she knew that even this was wrong and that Leda was not gone. She couldn't be.

Sarah could still hear the man in the truck. It was indecipherable noise from here.

Sarah walked up a slight incline, and at the top of the rise she caught her breath. A tent was in the woods, set away from the water, a pair of feet sticking out like those of that dead wicked witch in Oz. But these feet were wearing muddied work boots and clearly belonged to a man.

She felt a jolt of fear that was also familiarly reviving. She tried to keep her focus on the tranquil blue and muddied shadows of the lake, the reflection of so many trees. But:

She'd stood up to that mugger; what a profoundly stupid move.

And yet.

Fuck that, she'd yelled. What a rush of pride, what a spike of exhilaration. *Fuck you*.

She heard the truck gunning its engine and driving away. She kept walking at a rapid clip, on edge about strangers and how a hopeful or maybe just frankly entitled part of her always wanted to see people as better than they actually were.

The spot she finally found to set up at, without too many rocks and reeds, was farther away than she'd anticipated, and she hoped such a long walk wouldn't bother anyone. She'd offer to hold Sylvie while Kiki took a swim. She'd lay the baby down and point at trees and rocks and moss. She'd name everything in sight.

Hearing her group approach, she felt a familiar disappointment at the quiet being breached before she was ready. Even when Leda was little and Sarah truly missed her daughter during the day—no matter how she longed for Leda or looked forward to having dinner with Matthew—her heart sank when she turned the key in the lock and heard anyone was already home.

"Welcome to the country," said Arman, the first to emerge up the hill. "What a refuge."

"Shh," Kiki said, carrying Sylvie on her hip. "Just let it go."

"I just can't believe they get mugged and come here, they come to us for some peace, and we take them to a lake with a noisy drunk."

"Did you see the bumper sticker?" Sarah asked.

Arman nodded. "What a fucking relief they left. They are gone, right?"

Matthew peered through the trees toward the parking area. "Yeah, they're gone."

"Whew," said Sarah.

"He wasn't that bad," Matthew muttered.

"Oh no?" Sarah blurted, sharper than necessary. "Really?"

"No." Matthew took off his shirt as if to spite her, with not only his nonchalance but also his still fairly novel runner's physique. Then he turned and trudged through a bunch of weeds and dove right into the water.

"Are you okay?" Kiki asked her.

"Fine. Why? Do I sound angry?"

Kiki nodded.

"I don't mean to."

"You seem upset."

"Not to me," Arman said. "I mean, at least no more upset than she normally seems."

"Thanks, Arman. Thanks a million. Hey"—Sarah touched Kiki's shoulder and summoned up her least defensive voice— "I'm not upset. It's so nice to be here." Sarah kept an eye on Matthew and called out to him, "Hey. How's the water?"

In the silence that followed, Sylvie made several sounds as if she were testing each one and seeing which she liked best. She landed on a kind of mmmnnnmph, which she repeated until Sarah asked once more how the water was, and when Matthew pretended again not to hear her and stuck his head under, Sarah felt a dual twist of irritation and fear.

"I mean, you were mugged yesterday," Kiki now rushed to say. "It makes sense you'd be jumpy."

"Day before," Sarah muttered. "We were mugged the day before yesterday. The evening before, I guess."

"Okay then, the day *before* yesterday. It just happened, is my point. I only mean to say—it's been so long since I've seen you, so I don't know—"

"You don't know if I'm always like this."

"That's not what I meant." Kiki laughed; it sounded only a little bit forced. "I know I said I love that you're a misanthrope, but I didn't mean that either."

"You don't love it so much?"

"No, it's just that I don't think you're a misanthrope. I think you actually like people. You just don't always admit it when you do." Kiki shrugged. "Oh, and Heather and Karim wanted to make sure I passed along a goodbye."

Sarah nodded. "Byyyyyyye," she said, with a little wave. "Bye, guys!"

Kiki cracked a smile.

Then Sarah said to Sylvie, "Hi, *baby*," with what sounded even to her own ears like manic affection. "Where's Sylvie?" Sarah placed her hands over her eyes. When she took her hands away, Sylvie—bless her—gave a bright smile, and Sarah repeated this routine several times, buzzed from that simple smile again and again and again.

"You're allowed to stop," Kiki said.

"I forgot how much fun that is," Sarah said. "I love a good peekaboo."

Arman swooped up Sylvie and planted a kiss on her belly, at which Sylvie laughed even harder.

"Way to upstage me," Sarah said.

Matthew had swum pretty far out.

"Why don't you both go in?" Sarah asked them. "I'll hold Sylvie. If she'll have me."

Arman handed her over, and Sylvie turned instantly miserable, squirming in Sarah's arms.

"That's okay, sweetheart," Sarah told a crying Sylvie. "I get it."

Kiki reached out a bit too eagerly to take Sylvie back. Matthew might not have mentioned to Kiki that Sarah had lied about Leda, but Kiki's pale eyes looked wary, regardless. Or maybe the wariness was only exhaustion; Sarah couldn't tell.

"Well, in that case"—Sarah took off her shorts and T-shirt—"who's joining me?"

A hushed and matrimonial back-and-forth ensued about who should stay, so Sarah tuned them out and waded in, walking instead of swimming. With her feet immersed in the sandy, then rocky, then mucky bottom, she let each part of her be submerged until she could no longer stand. She swam freestyle for a stretch before looking up and getting her bearings. The truck was gone. Only three cars remained: Matthew and Sarah's, Kiki and Arman's, and the dried-blood wreck. In the other direction was Matthew. She tried to keep him at twelve o'clock; she did the butterfly as if being tested.

"Fancy," said Arman, treading water behind her, the next time she came up for air.

"I was on the swim team in high school." This made him laugh. "I'm just saying . . . you know, later? When it's time to pick teams?"

"I won't forget."

They treaded water in silence for a while.

"So your friends left," she said.

"They did. Thank God."

"As soon as we drive off, you'll say that about us, too."

"Probably."

She splashed him, laughing, and he splashed her back. They went back and forth a few more rounds, each time with too much gusto.

They stopped splashing and settled into watching Matthew in the distance. "Do you think he's swimming the whole way across?" Arman asked.

She strained to see Matthew's head bobbing up and down or the ripples of his body slicing through the water and wondered what would happen if Matthew got a cramp. He was so far away; how would anyone get to him fast enough? Despite not actually feeling anxious about this, she said, "I'm getting anxious about him swimming so far."

"He's in really good shape," Arman replied, acknowledging how true this was with somewhat begrudging admiration.

"So you're saying I shouldn't worry?"

"That's right. No worrying. Dude's a beast."

"Would you swim out that far?" she asked.

"Maybe."

"You wouldn't."

"No?"

She shook her head, sank under the water for a moment. When she broke the surface, she said, "You don't need to."

"What does that mean?"

"It means you don't need to run or swim miles at a time to know you're strong."

"Oh, I get it."

"What?"

"You don't think I'm in good enough condition to swim that far."

"I'm not saying that!"

"Come on, you are, too."

"Arman!" She was treading water and blushing. "You know you're in good shape. You don't need me to tell you that."

"Maybe I do."

"Well, you shouldn't."

"Okay, fine. I shouldn't." He splashed water hard, but not at her. "Let's go." Arman started to swim.

"Um, no thanks."

"Come on, Sarah. *You're* in good shape!"

"Oh, please."

"You were on the swim team!"

He swam away. After a moment, she followed, but Matthew had evidently come to his senses and was now headed toward them. They silently decided to all make their way back to Kiki, doing enough of a swim in one long stretch that when Sarah finally came up for a break, it took a moment to get oriented. Matthew and Arman were standing farther in toward shore, already engrossed in conversation. She did a quiet breaststroke toward them and floated on her back, pretending to be relaxed.

"It's the phones," she heard Matthew say.

"Sure." Arman nodded.

"They go for the phones more than money or cards. It's an easy way to make substantial cash."

Sarah felt a stab of fear. She recalled the shock of her hands hitting the ground, the sting of breaking her fall.

"Traffickers," continued Matthew, "that's what they call them. They resell them overseas."

"*Traffickers?*" Arman grinned. "Seems like a strong term for someone who resells a phone."

"Oh, it's trafficking. Huge profits. Something like a billion a year."

"I mean, I know they're doing this whole scam with the warranty-exchange programs, but—"

"Did you both hear the same piece on NPR or something?" Sarah asked, squinting into the afternoon sun, barely keeping aggravation at bay. Since when did Matthew know anything about cell phone trafficking?

"I'm just angry still," Matthew said.

Angry? Oh, really?

If anything, over the last twenty-four hours he seemed to have perfected tranquility. He'd tempered her lingering fury with every small gesture and comment, and when he wasn't doing so, she'd felt it anyway. He'd handed over his belongings and tried to hand over hers. What more would he have given over had the mugger demanded it? He had no more fight left. Or maybe he'd never had any to start. She'd lied about Leda—yes, fine, she'd lied—but she was also the one who'd fight to get her back. Matthew was letting her go. Sarah knew he was. And he'd also essentially allowed a man to shove his wife to the ground.

Angry?

Please.

She dove underwater with her heart pounding too hard and questioned how exactly so much fury toward Matthew was justified. She had no answers, none at all, as she swam back out as fast as she could into where she could no longer stand. She passed where Kiki and Sylvie were sitting in the sand, back in the direction of the cars and where the trail began. She swam for what must have been ten minutes before she saw another sandy bank. She waded up to it. She could hardly see the path through the tall weeds.

When she emerged from the weeds in the shade of the woods, she shuddered to see the tent on the other side of the path. She looked away quickly and should have shot right back in the water. She should have swum toward Kiki and Sylvie. She understood this, but she didn't. Even as she was moving forward, it was clear she was headed in the wrong direction.

A jumble of blankets spilled out of the tent, amid the remnants of a campfire, several empty beer cans. She stood at the mouth of the tent, but the feet weren't sticking out anymore. She wondered if the man had gone for a walk or swim, or maybe the pathetic car that looked as if it hadn't started in several seasons was actually his car and maybe it did start. Maybe he'd driven away from this, his home base. Maybe he worked a construction job. Maybe the man with the boots sticking out of the tent was a neo-Nazi skinhead who romanticized Old Dixie while growing up in the sticks of upstate New York and had his very own mini–Confederate flag that he'd whip out of his pocket at any moment. Or maybe this tent belonged to an illegal immigrant, ready to work but too frightened to live anywhere in the open anymore and thus reduced to living in the woods.

When she realized he was right in front of her, standing behind a tree farther back from the path, she forgot her imaginary scenarios. Here was a dark-haired guy with ruddy cheeks. Tall; light eyes.

"Can't a man piss in the woods anymore?"

Her stomach dropped. Her wet hair trickled a barely audible patter on the dead, dry leaves. She looked down at the water speckling the leaves, seeping into the ground. A worm worked its way through a particularly moist patch.

"Hey—" he nearly shouted.

Why didn't she bolt? It was as if she were just another tree: solid bark, gnarled roots. She looked away, and when she thought about how she was wearing only her navy two-piece, she trained her eyes on the surface of the lake, as if it were imperative she find a hidden code in its reflection. She heard him coming closer, ostensibly returning to his tent. She tugged at the skimpy seat of her suit (*It's cheeky*, said the salesgirl in a killer Scottish brogue, and Sarah had been done for). She'd charged an absurd sum of money on her AmEx for a swimsuit, a bag made from a grain sack, and a pair of exceptionally dark sunglasses as if she were headed to Switzerland to get her eyes done. She'd shopped and packed for her trip to see Leda all in one day, with the same delusional spirit she'd donned her nicer blouses and taken time with her makeup over the last several years for a visit to the gynecologist or dermatologist, as if (after a pretty heavy-duty basal cell carcinoma and two irregular Pap smears a few years back) such preparations might ward off death. She'd called Matthew on the way to the airport to tell him where she was going. He didn't pick up—he was in Mongolia doing an ad shoot for T-Mobile—she couldn't keep the time difference straight; she left a voice message, explaining.

She'd packed up that cheeky suit and gone off to Baja. She never once went swimming; that day on the beach with the wild horses had been the closest she'd come. She'd spent most of her time in the shade under a huge open-air *palapa*, shivering while listening to Leda. Her daughter spoke reluctantly, like a celebrity with whom Sarah, having outbid everyone else at a charity auction, had won the opportunity to have breakfast. Thin people came and went under the *palapa*. The gray cement floor was freezing; she could feel it through the soles of her flip-flops. The warm sun beckoned right outside of where they were sitting, shining on the pale gravel path that led to a scattershot cactus garden and high walls festooned with fuchsia bougain-villea and topped with spikes of broken glass. But where she sat with Leda, the shade took on the cat-piss smell of fresh papaya and vitamins. Sarah was starving but afraid that if she mentioned something as mundane as food, Leda would stop talking.

Leda talked about the beach's sand and how it looked white from afar but stubbornly clung to everyone's skin in a faint gal-axy of black and silver. Leda talked about writing a children's book, or really—she corrected herself—the book was writing itself, flowing through her, and that everything positive from her life was pouring directly onto the page. *What was positive?* Sarah couldn't help but ask, but Leda didn't answer. Instead she devolved into aphorisms—nothing that made particular sense, nothing that Sarah would ever remember. There was a dawn walk with Leda to the top of a cliff. They sat in meditation. When Sarah opened her eyes, morning had shattered the oyster sky and Leda was already standing. They drove to a farm down a narrow dirt road. They got out of the truck and stretched. The clear white, lavender, yellow light—the light itself, the way it shone on Leda, the way it suggested, well, grace—it kept making Sarah weep. *You've got to stop crying*, said Leda, while swatting flies off a goat she adored. The Leader (whom Sarah never met) had made an arrangement with a local farmer. The Members tended his farm in exchange for plenty of goat milk. Sarah wanted to know why he needed so many people tending his small farm, and if maybe there was more to the exchange, but she never had the nerve to ask.

"CAN'T A MAN take a *fucking piss?*"

"Of course," she said, startled now, even scared. "I'm sorry."

He bent down to pick up a blanket. The way he moved reminded her of people in ski boots: motion stunted but also filled with intent. He might have been a former athlete. He looked rougher than that, but she could picture it. He shook out one of the cruddy blankets.

"It's okay," he said, in a surprisingly conversational tone. "I'm just kidding. Really. I was kidding. I didn't mean to scare you."

"I wasn't scared."

"Yeah, you were. You were." He gave a crooked smile. "Hey, you did invade my campsite."

"It's right here on the path. You might want to consider pitching your tent somewhere more private next time."

He interlaced his hands and stretched them out in front of him. "Ever been here before?"

She shook her head. "It's beautiful."

He shrugged, looking her over. "It's all right." She didn't want to catch him in the act of looking so she remained focused on the water. "You get into some kind of accident recently?"

She instinctively covered her face with her hand.

"You fought with someone? You got into it?"

"Right." She sort of laughed.

He didn't laugh at all. "Someone hurt you?"

"It wasn't—I mean—"

"Someone hurt you."

She nodded slowly.

"I'm sorry to hear it."

"Oh. Well, thanks."

He nodded. Put his hands in his pockets.

She hurried to fill the ensuing silence: "So what else you got?"

"About what?"

She laughed. "Me, I guess."

"You have a husband," he said without hesitation.

She nodded, unexpectedly excited that he was playing her game.

"You have a baby."

She felt herself nodding. "Wait, how did you guess that?"

"Boy or girl?"

"Girl. Eight months."

"You sure bounced back."

A bird made a sudden racket in the trees; she looked up

at the last moment of flapping wings and disrupted leaves. A twig fell to the ground. He seemed perfectly comfortable looking straight at her and—for the moment—not saying anything more.

"I saw you last night," he finally said.

"You *saw me*? When?"

"You were outside with your friends. And then with your husband in the middle of the night." His tone went more serious. "To be honest, I'd started to wonder if you really existed. I mean, I'd never laid eyes on you before then."

"Before—?"

"I'm in the house across the creek," he finally explained. "I'm just camping out here for a night or so. I came to watch the sunrise."

Her mind started racing but landed on the fact that he was the neighbor with the flashlight, the flag. She remembered that Kiki had never met him.

"Wow," she said. "Right. Sometimes I have trouble sleeping. I mean—"

"The baby."

She nodded. She wanted to ask if he had kids, but she had sworn she would never ask anyone that question ever again.

"You're renting the McCann house."

She didn't answer.

"Let me guess: The two of you wanted to get away from the city. You wanted something cheaper, some country livin'. New baby and all."

Despite his sarcasm, despite, obviously, none of this being true, she resumed nodding.

"What's the baby's name?"

She shook her head. Not that.

"Oh, come on, neighbor. What's the name?"

"Do you live here? Here in the woods?"

He shook his head. "I got a house. I just told you that."

"I'm sorry. I didn't catch if you actually lived there or were, you know, maybe visiting?"

"No, it's my house."

"Oh, okay. That's funny then, right? I mean, that's a coincidence."

He shrugged. "Summer." As if that explained anything.

"Summer's over. Though you'd never know it."

"I don't like the heat. You?"

"I don't mind it. I prefer heat to cold."

"Do you now?" He laughed.

"Yeah, I do."

"That's too bad."

"Why?"

"I just bet you look cute in a snow hat."

"Um"—she blushed—"not at all. I don't have a good hat face. My features are too small."

He shook his head. "Anyway, that's when I come here." He looked at her straight on. "You know, when it's hot. I like to hide out a bit."

She realized she'd been standing stock-still. Her knees were hyperextended. Her legs were aching. "I'm hiding, too."

"Is that right?"

Why, she wondered, was she doing this? Did she think a series of shocks would somehow bring her back to life? She envisioned herself as a golem; it was easy. She might be disguised as a well-maintained formerly creative person who had a taste for fine textiles and cocktails and expensive organic hair dye, but she was actually a lifeless block of clay, with stones for eyes and a big gaping hole for a mouth. It was as if she'd just discovered a new rift and it was expanding by the second. What would you do if you found a hole in yourself? You'd fill it. You would stuff it up with whatever crude materials you happened to have on hand.

Even if it made no sense?

Her heart and pulse were going off now—like at the park at dusk two nights ago, like her phone ringing with a number she didn't recognize.

Even if it made no sense.

"You're hiding?" He folded the blanket. She thought of soldiers folding the flag. Why was precision so moving?

She nodded, her heart speeding. A man around Sarah's age, new to the support group, had an identical-twin brother who had recently died. What the twin had: a history littered with dirty needles, blood poisoning, heart problems, and a pacemaker that had clocked the rhythms of his heart leading straight up to his death. Those numbers had spiked outrageously high in several bursts in a perfect mathematical illustration of the body's absorption of crack or cocaine. The man told the story week after week. He repeated the numbers, how high, how low. He wondered whether it was crack or cocaine he'd taken that final time, then wondered why he wondered when it didn't matter, nothing did.

"You're hiding," he repeated. "Dressed like that."

She nodded.

"Who're you hiding from?"

"My husband."

"Your husband?"

She continued to nod.

She could feel his eyes all over her skin, looking for bruises and finding them. The one on her thigh was purple today, big as a newborn's head. The cut on the bridge of her nose had started to heal, its blood beginning to dry and scab, which made it look worse.

He leaned against a tree and looked at her.

Her body was, she thought, plain. Not homely plain, more like . . . stark. She'd been called graceful, but graceful implied willowy, and that wasn't her. *You have the type of look men freakin' love*, her friend Andrea's mother had told her during their senior year of high school. And when she responded, *What do you mean?* she'd been told, *You look your best when you come out of the shower—you're naturally pretty. But, honey*, Andrea's mother had said (kind of cruelly, Sarah realized in retrospect), *the flip side of your kind of pretty? There's no surprise to symmetry. You always look the same.*

"You have, like, no tits," the man said, still leaning on the tree. But then he muttered something else she couldn't hear, with a tone that suggested some kind of deep approval. The path was right between them. At any moment, anyone might or might not come along.

She said nothing. She didn't avert her gaze.

"What's with you? You do something wrong?"

"Why?"

He laughed. "You have a guilty face. What'd you do?"

"Nothing."

"C'mon, what'd you do?"

Was she losing it? Why now? She suddenly loved being alive with surprising—even desperate—conviction. She was too attached to her husband and her daughter. She felt incredible despair several times a day. But she'd never feared being actually unstable. Where Leda's instability came from Sarah did not know, but this was the first moment she considered it could be her.

"You want something?" he asked hoarsely.

Still she didn't back away or dive into the lake.

He was moving toward her, across the path.

"Don't touch me," she said calmly, her voice low.

"Don't touch you?"

"That's right."

He came closer. She could smell his sweat—loamy, woodsy, but maybe ketchup, too?—and also something like embers, the morning after a fire.

She'd been flirting with Arman. But it had been harmless. Hadn't it?

She was standing by a tree and he put his hand on that tree. He leaned in to her. She hadn't removed her suit but she felt as if she had. She wasn't scared or angry or sad. In the absence of those more familiar sensations, there was a hollowing out that extended to her head, a rush of air like a plane taking off. This, she remembered. This, she could do. She was a breezeway with a door about to slam. He leaned even closer. She could feel the heat coming off his chest like that of a sweaty wiry dog, and she could tell that he was hard, she could feel it brush against her thigh. Inside her head, on a loop: the same word she'd invented five years ago after attending an introduction to Transcendental Meditation and balking at the idea of paying for a mantra.

When he put his fingers on the ridge of her wet bathing-suit bottom, when he pulled the elastic back just the slightest bit, she said, "Stop," and shoved his hand away.

He took his hand back and crossed his arms at his chest. She watched him breathing evenly, not embarrassed or defensive. She stood amid the dead, dry leaves and wet earth and he towered above her. She knew he could do whatever he wanted, and this excited him and it excited her, too, because she knew she was not going to let him.

Then—from far away, almost inaudibly—"Sarah?"

When she shouted, "Hi!," her eyes were still locked with his.

Then he silently backed away, crossed the path, and headed to his tent.

She ran in Kiki's direction. Sarah saw her in the distance and she seemed to be alone.

Sarah would have to pass by this tent, this man, on their way out—they all would.

"Kiki," she shouted, "Kiki!" Sarah hurried toward her, smiling, smiling, smiling. "*Hi*—hi, what's going on?"

"Are you okay?"

"Am I okay? I'm fine! It's so beautiful here. Don't you think it's beautiful?"

Kiki was looking both at and beyond her, as if Kiki could sense that something strange might have just taken place. *I mean*, she could imagine Kiki whispering to Arman about her, *the years have not been kind.*

"Let me hold Sylvie." Sarah walked Kiki back in the direction of their outing spot in the sun. "Have a swim, please."

"You know you're shivering, right?"

"I'm not cold." In a sudden burst of sadness, Sarah threw an arm around Kiki. "Really." Sarah continued to walk with Kiki awkwardly crushed into her side. "I'd tell you."

"You wouldn't," Kiki responded lightly.

"Of course I would. Why wouldn't I tell you if I was cold?"

"Because you want me to get in that water. Because you want me to feel the freedom you felt when you had the chance to swim away." Kiki stopped and looked up at Sarah with her big gray eyes. "You're generous like that. Or needy." Kiki forced a laugh. "Or . . . something. I don't know anymore." She looked down, fidgeted with a button on her gauzy and somehow fashionably tattered dress. "I don't know. It's been such a long time since we've really talked so I don't want to speak out of turn, but—"

"Can we take a walk?" Sarah interrupted.

"Aren't we doing that?"

"I mean a longer one."

"I don't know. Sylvie will need to—"

"Can't Arman take her?" Sarah knew she sounded impatient, which she was, and her heart was still racing from the thought of that man, with his flesh and bone and muscle and blood and how she'd let him touch her.

She hadn't exactly wanted that man. But she hadn't wanted to scream.

"Fine." Kiki's unembellished tone made Sarah realize that up until this moment Kiki had been faking something. "Fine. We'll pass by them without stopping. We can't stop. If Sylvie sees me, I'll get sucked in."

They walked in silence, finding the same rhythm.

"Why do you keep turning around?" Kiki asked.

"I don't."

"Did you see that tent back there when we walked from the cars?"

Sarah's stomach dropped before she nodded.

Kiki nodded. They were both quiet for a while. "I hate it here," Kiki finally said.

"You—"

"Hate it," Kiki snapped. "I hate it."

"At the lake or . . . ?"

"Here. Living here."

"Oh," Sarah said dumbly. "But I thought—"

Kiki put her fingers to her lips as they approached a familiar stand of trees. As they crept along silently, Sarah looked through the skein of branches toward the lake. Arman stood on the sand, facing the water. Matthew sat on a towel, drying in the sun. Arman must have been holding Sylvie, but with his back to the woods it was hard to tell. From this vantage, with the sun bouncing off the water and casting a golden blur, it might have been twenty years ago; they all took the train to Long Beach once, early on a Sunday morning. Right now, the years might mix together and a five-year-old Leda might just pop out of the water and demand a towel. Or an eight-year-old Leda could ask to hold Sylvie by herself; Matthew would show her how.

They walked swiftly past their husbands. The woods became denser, the path less clearly defined. They walked in silence long enough that it felt awkward to break that silence.

"Why are you living here?" Sarah finally spoke.

Kiki didn't stop walking, but Sarah had the feeling Kiki was about to. "It's cheap."

"But surely you could rent something in—"

"When's the last time you tried to rent an apartment?" Kiki sped up again.

"Why does everyone talk to me like I don't know anything?"

Sarah could have sworn she heard Kiki stifle a laugh.

"Are you *laughing*?"

"No. I'm not." It was true: she didn't look amused. "Sarah."

"*What*?"

"You have never really worked."

"Excuse me?"

"You've never worked."

Sarah felt her face go hot. Her eyes started to itch. "Do you have any idea what it takes to make a film?"

"That's not what I'm talking ab—"

"Plus, I teach."

"Okay." Kiki shook her head. "But you know what I mean."

Sarah gritted her teeth. She felt the enamel scraping.

"I'm not saying you're not talented and extremely compelling. I'm saying—"

"So," Sarah interrupted, "I know I don't know anything about how your life has been." She stopped walking and Kiki did, too. "Just like," Sarah said, against her better judgment, "you don't know about mine. And I know"—Sarah hesitated—"I know I'm really bad at keeping in touch." She shook her head. "You're so good at it."

"Please don't say that."

"What? You *are* good at it."

"I really, *really* hate when people say that. It's like saying someone is good at making small talk. No one *likes* to make small talk—"

"Who said anything about small talk?"

"People make small talk to be polite. And being polite is about making other people feel comfortable."

"Who's talking about being polite?"

"I am." Kiki suddenly sounded furious. "I am talking about it. Is that okay with you?"

Sarah nodded.

"I am talking about the fact that no one is good at keeping in touch. It's not a skill like playing the piano or drawing. People either need one another and care enough to take the time to express that need or they don't."

"But—"

"What?"

Sarah sat down on a rock.

"*What?* I tried keeping in touch with you because you were my best friend. Did you know that? That when I was in my late twenties you were my best friend? Does that sound immature to you? My *best friend*. Like I was in seventh grade?"

"No," sputtered Sarah, "no, of course not—"

"When you blew me off for the—who could keep track?—eighth time? I finally got the point."

Sarah wanted to throw her arms around Kiki and beg her

forgiveness. Sarah wanted to tell her everything. "But I didn't," Sarah said instead. "I didn't blow you off."

"Yes, you did. And that's okay. I mean, now it is. For some reason that still isn't fully clear to me, I just had to let you know about Sylvie. And I wanted to see you again, I really did, but—"

"I'm *so* glad you did. I'm so grateful you got in touch—"

"Good. But just be straight with me, at least about your life. Or at least about the past."

Sarah nodded. "Okay." Why couldn't she come up with anything more honest? *You were my best friend, too!* It went through her head like music from a passing car.

She remembered exactly the last time that Kiki had left a message on her voice mail. Kiki was so sympathetic and unpetty by nature, didn't keep track of who did what in friendships. But her voice on the recording started to have an undertone of hurt and maybe anger, and Leda was seventeen and had just gotten caught with a substantial stash of pot and a small stash of heroin, and she might have been dealing pot, and Sarah couldn't imagine talking to anyone about anything, and, *no, Matthew, no, not even Kiki.* Even while being annoyed with Kiki's tone on the voice messages, Sarah knew it was unfair of her to be annoyed. It would, she reasoned, be impossible for anyone to hear how Leda's senior year in high school was unfolding and to not at least partially blame the parents or certainly the mother. Even as Sarah felt completely blindsided and not to blame, she had to be. Who wouldn't think that? How could she fault people? She was the mother. She was to blame.

Kiki also left messages for Leda, who (as far as Sarah knew) never called Kiki back either. Lying to Leda, Sarah maintained that she and Kiki spoke all the time. How Sarah wished now that had been the case. She nagged Leda to return Kiki's calls; it was just one more thing they fought about.

Kiki called a month later. *I'm just wondering*—her voice was pitched high while speaking out into what had to now seem like the ether—*if everything is okay? I'm just parked in the Erewhon lot. I'm realizing I bought too much yogurt again, and, I don't know, I thought I'd try you.*

Then the years went by.

Sarah wondered about the man and woman on the lakeside. She imagined that same fleshy woman drying off, pulling on a shirt. She'd light a cigarette with a plastic lighter. She'd take her sweet-ass time. Who had decided it was time to go home? Was she a wife, a girlfriend? Did those two belong to each other or were they barely acquainted? *Hey, baby, let me teach you how to swim.*

The man with the tent seemed imaginary. He couldn't have—for instance—stuck two fingers under the waistband of her bikini bottom.

"We're broke," Kiki said.

"Broke?"

Kiki nodded.

"When you say *broke*—"

"We're broke, Sarah. Broke. In massive debt, actually. I have to sort things out. And it just—" Kiki started pacing. "Look—I make a small salary from my textile company and Arman has work—don't get me wrong, he's working and I'm kicking it into higher gear and he's always got something about to drop but—" Kiki's eyes were saucers, truly gray. And with her curly hair spilling out of a scarf, her pale skin, and her freckled forearms wrapped around her waist as if she might just go ahead and retch—

"Kiki. What . . . happened?"

"You mean, 'Why are you so broke?' Is that what you're asking?"

"I mean, I guess I am."

"Listen to me—oh my God, I'm so sorry. I'm being ridiculous." Kiki's hands fluttered in front of her face, as if she were about to sneeze or cry.

Sarah remembered how Kiki had lit candles one Friday evening; she had looked strikingly similar then to how she did now. Kiki had explained to Leda how she waved her hands three times to welcome the Sabbath Queen.

"We'll work it out." Kiki nodded. She finally opened her eyes. "We both just have unpredictable careers and we always have. Or at least Arman always has. I've just had—y'know—*low-paying* careers. Look at your face—I'm sorry I'm venting! You bring out this . . . honesty in me. I'm really sorry."

"Stop apologizing." Sarah heard such blunt echoes of Leda in her own voice. *You've got to stop crying.* Whose impatience had come first?

"We'll work it out."

"I'm sure you will but—"

"Having Sylvie has just made me think about everything differently. Obviously. But I have to take it down a notch. According to Arman, I have to have a little faith."

Sarah thought of Arman in the car last night, sitting at the table with his head in his hands. Was this the source of his unhappiness? Money trouble? She was ashamed how disappointed she felt. She'd anticipated—hoped for?—real betrayal.

Kiki started walking again and Sarah followed. The path narrowed so they were single file.

"It's not easy," Sarah said.

"What part?"

"Oh, I don't know. The chilling out? The having faith?"

Kiki reached for a low-hanging branch. Sarah thought she was going to pull on it in a burst of frustration, but she only pushed it gently aside and made way for Sarah to pass.

"I wanted a baby," Kiki said, while still holding on to the branch. "I wanted to be pregnant."

Sarah didn't dare say anything. If she let her be, Kiki would eventually continue.

"At some point we stopped trying. Then we tried to adopt. We ended up in a foster-to-adopt situation about four years ago in L.A. He was about the same age when he came to us as Sylvie is now. We wanted to adopt him and we thought it was going to happen. It almost happened. But he went back to his mother, who's a heroin addict."

Sarah bit the inside of her chewed-up mouth; she felt a flash of searing pain.

"She's an addict but she's still his mother," Kiki added. "I mean, of course."

Sarah nodded.

"I happen to know she's still using. He was ours for eleven months. Now he's living with a drug addict. Can you imagine?"

Of course Sarah could. She imagined Leda's teeth yellowed and her arms scarred and her toes mangled and her belly a perfect orb. She could imagine being granted Leda's baby, and she could imagine Leda coming back for that baby and disappearing forever.

Kiki was still holding on to the branch.

"What's his name?" Sarah asked. "The boy."

"Joseph. We called him Joe." Kiki let the branch go, but she didn't start walking again.

"Oh, Kiki." Naturally Kiki would be an extraprotective mother—after what she'd gone through, how could she not be? Sarah reached for Kiki's hand, pulled her into a hug. "I'm just really sorry."

"I'm so happy now." Kiki started to cry and pulled away. "I mean, I'm still worried about Joe and it makes me so sad to imagine that maybe I will actually, you know, *stop* worrying about him one day, but I'm also just . . . happy." She sniffled. "And I know it's not feminist or liberated or whatever to say that my life would be incomplete without my child, but it would be. It would be *one hundred percent* incomplete without Sylvie." Kiki's usually soft demeanor morphed into something fierce and maybe even threatening. Even her rounded cheeks and shoulders took on a sharper form. "I'm sure—somehow I'm just *sure*—that you understand this. So, you know, I would do it all again. I would. But I messed up. I mean, I really, really, really messed up."

"You're in debt?"

Kiki nodded.

"Insurance didn't cover the IVF?"

Kiki laughed darkly. "It covered the first three times. There were—um—more."

"I'm so sorry."

They heard Sylvie crying from far away and picked up their pace, heading back. These weren't particularly worrying cries, but still, they started to run. When they reached the spit of sand, they were both out of breath. Sarah thought, *Two men would never have done that.* Why had they run? Before she was even settled in Kiki's arms, Sylvie immediately went quiet.

"Nice walk?" Arman asked.

Sarah could tell Matthew was avoiding her. He wouldn't meet her eye. He was a good person, but as Sarah chastised herself for having been unfairly hostile toward him earlier, she was only besieged by more anger.

We'll wait was what Matthew always said. And after their same sad back-and-forth, his tone would inevitably harden: *We will wait for her to come back to us, but we won't wait to live our lives.*

Despite their having run through the woods and being out of breath, the edge of the heat had clearly smoothed itself out; it was time to get going. "What time is it?" Sarah asked. Arman's impressively large waterproof watch was evidently broken. Because if it worked, wouldn't they have sold it? If they were truly broke? "What time is it?" she repeated, but no one knew; no one was rushing to check a phone.

"Not sure," Kiki finally replied.

They slowly gathered the towels and bags and started for the car. As they walked closer to the tent, Sarah started sweating profusely. She didn't allow herself to look anywhere besides the ground just in front of her. It was as if, instead of this basic trail, she were on a treacherous nighttime hike; she became intensely focused on where to place her feet, hearing, *Hey, hey, HEY.*

She turned to look, but no one was there. No one had called out to her.

Yet she'd heard this deep searching voice, its muted desire, its timbre, just as she'd heard Leda crying in the night long after she was a baby. No witch feet were sticking out, no stranger, though the tent remained.

As they stepped out of the shaded woods and walked toward the cars, Sarah started to feel a strange pulsing in her left temple, as if a migraine were in her future, but she'd never had a migraine. She'd forgotten to apply bug repellent, and her ankles and forearms were suddenly afire with small but potent mosquito bites. She'd already scratched hard enough to draw blood. She knew the man from the tent—the *neighbor*—could show up at any moment. The man on the train popped into her head or, rather, more like floated by her eyes and whispered into both ears. This odd old man from Prague had been meeting her grief and recklessness with something like a warning.

You are a good mother, he'd said.

"I'm sorry," said Sarah loudly, "but I really need to get out of here. Can we pick up the pace?"

"We're moving," said Matthew. "Relax."

"I'm getting ravaged by mosquitoes." Sarah realized she had to get them all to leave the lake before the neighbor showed up. "No one else is getting bitten?" she asked Kiki and Arman irritably, frantically scratching her legs and ankles.

Matthew grabbed her arm and—more than the fear of how she'd behaved with the man in the woods who could have assaulted her, more than that she'd pretty much encouraged him to do so, more than the thug who'd shoved her to the ground and stolen her bag and her wallet and her phone with the number that Leda could dial if she ever changed her mind and came back to them—Matthew's grip made her furious.

"Give me the keys," Sarah insisted, shaking off his grip.

"*Hang on,*" Matthew said.

Kiki and Arman picked up their pace and passed them by, obviously aware of their arguing.

"Just give them to me," Sarah whispered as they approached the cars. "There's room for you in their front seat."

"Look." Matthew stopped her, putting his hands on her shoulders. "You need—" He paused, as if phrasing mattered. As if he were measuring out gin and scooping up ice and thinking about how, if he handled this correctly, they could all get home without tension here and without any fighting in the car. They could get back to the house with enough time to shower, enough hours in the evening to mention the unexpected beauty of the lake, how good Sylvie was, how far Matthew had swum. They could reflect upon a perfect day as they sipped gin and tonics with lime.

"You need to settle down," whispered Matthew.

Sarah kicked sand at Matthew's feet. The kick was small, just a little spray of sand, but it proved he was right; she was acting like a child. But as she saw Kiki securing Sylvie in her car seat, as she saw this smart reaction—the *right* reaction—to her childish animosity toward Matthew, she felt a wave of not caring about anything. She felt grateful that Kiki was doing what she'd asked and that they were getting going quickly, but this gratitude was abstract. She was a great mother, Kiki, a natural. She was in the car, focused on her child. Aside from these somehow detached observations, Sarah felt only aggravation. She kept scanning the woods for the man. She wondered if he was watching. Then she noticed that the decrepit car was gone.

Her relief transformed into the sudden understanding that Matthew looked truly nervous. She knew he was disturbed by her unpredictability since the mugging, and it occurred to Sarah that he was perhaps not actually optimistic and centered, the way she'd always assumed. Maybe, contrary to what she and the old foreign man from the subway had agreed upon, people *don't* actually change, and Matthew was still the young man she'd met when she was twenty years old, the one who'd been—up until right before they'd met—unable to speak in public. Maybe her husband was so agreeable and said yes so often not because he was magnanimous and hardworking but because he was driven by fear.

She brought her hand to Matthew's cheek.

He shook his head. Then he unlocked the car.

She watched him buckle his seat belt. Her husband. She watched him turn the key in the ignition. They followed Arman and Kiki's Honda. Part of her wanted to ask him to keep on driving. To drive past Kiki and Arman and Sylvie and never see them again. They could try somewhere different, something new. But she'd done that before—both with and without Matthew—and she understood now there was no such thing as new enough.

five

SUNDAY
EVENING

W HEN THEY CLIMBED THE STEPS OF THE
porch, there was the same humid air as the
previous evening. They'd arrived from the city
in the same spot just over twenty-four hours before, and it felt
as if time had become tangled. Sarah realized that she'd seen
this weekend as some kind of test, as if the past were no more

complicated than an exclusive club, and by reconnecting to Kiki and Arman, they might gain some access.

But in the aftermath of the day's outing, feeling both disappointed with herself and dizzyingly unmoored, she had what felt like a presentiment: Kiki and Arman would refuse to answer the door. No matter how much Sarah and Matthew knocked or how long they stood there, Kiki and Arman would turn up their music and ignore them. They would or wouldn't send out their bags. She could easily picture Arman doing a sweep of the guest room—tossing most items in the trash and the choice ones in a box for the basement. He and Kiki had been stoop-sale pros when they'd lived in Brooklyn, and Sarah pictured her soft cotton pants on a hanger with a sticker, her gold hoops displayed near the cashbox on a scarf-draped folding table.

As she knocked on the door one more time, she realized she might have tried to stick around to see how nervous that woman at the lake really was. She'd been laughing, sure, but there'd been something sinister about that man. Leda could be in a similarly volatile situation somewhere. Leda could be tethered to some jerk in the middle of the woods, and Sarah would not want a stranger to simply look the other way. She thought of one of the support group members. Still grief-stricken after a decade, the woman talked exclusively about her daughter, who'd been trying to get to the next level of whatever godforsaken course she was taking when the daughter had become gravely ill. Evidently she'd asked for medical attention and someone had read her the Vedas.

Just as she was about to suggest to Matthew that they walk into town and find any form of distraction, Arman opened the door and let them in. They followed him toward the living room. The air was stale. Kiki was on the floor with Sylvie, who was sitting up and smiling and waving her hands, happy to see them.

"I'm sorry," Sarah rushed to say, her voice suddenly choked with tears upon seeing Sylvie smile. "I'm sorry for being such a pill."

"It's no big deal." Arman shrugged, which, at least for now, was all the reassurance she needed.

"I mean—" Sarah stammered, "what even *happened* back there? Those mosquitoes really put me over the edge." She found herself searching their faces, wanting more than ever to connect.

"What happened?" Kiki repeated, with her eyes fixed on Sylvie, reaching for her fingers and making her giggle. "You were irritable. We can take it."

"How about a drink?" said Arman.

Everyone nodded.

He headed into the kitchen, and as Sarah watched him go, she wondered whom he'd been speaking to in his car in the middle of the night. She impulsively took Matthew's hand. Sometimes the urge to show him affection came on so strongly; she was always slightly surprised. If he had walked away before she could grab his hand, she would have followed her husband— the same husband toward whom she'd recently felt such anger, even hatred—across the room to touch him. They stood looking down at Kiki and Sylvie, who were passing a stuffed mouse back and forth.

"Sit down," said Kiki. "Now you're making me nervous."

"Sorry," Sarah said. She and Matthew sat down on the couch. "I'm sorry."

Kiki shrugged before pulling Sylvie onto her lap as she leaned against the base of a leather club chair.

Arman came out with a bottle of tequila, grapefruit juice, a bucket of ice, and four glasses. She loved how he hadn't asked what anyone wanted. This was exactly what she wanted. As he fixed the drinks, she offered a habitual silent prayer of gratitude that she was not an alcoholic and could therefore enjoy this drink. During Leda's first stint in rehab, she and Matthew had each taken a hard look at their habits, their history, and their families' histories. They'd browbeaten and theorized and she'd given up all alcohol for several months to see if she was secretly dependent, even though she had a low tolerance and rarely had more than some wine with dinner. After she was sufficiently sure that she wasn't addicted to alcohol, she gave up sugar, gluten, dairy, then finally welcomed it all back, deciding never to give up anything again unless there was an absolute medical necessity.

Sarah sat back on the couch. There was a prolonged moment of pouring and stirring; no one spoke. Kiki cuddled Sylvie. A tree branch scraped gently against the window screen; there was the repeated faraway honking of a horn. As Sarah's gaze traveled over everyone's heads and through the windows, she could see the stone wall and outdoor table; the leaves on the verdant trees. She let her vision narrow and all she saw was green. She could feel the man's fingers almost gentle on her stomach, the twilight of the park two nights ago now as her face hit the ground.

She touched the cut on the bridge of her nose.

"What'd they take?" asked Kiki.

"What?" Sarah asked, confused.

"When you were mugged."

"I told you." Sarah was perfectly aware she had no business being irritated, that if there was any moment to let details slide, it was now. "My phone."

"That's it?"

"I have a lot on my phone."

"No backup?"

Sarah took a longer drink. "No, not really."

"You mean like notes? Did you lose notes?"

Sarah nodded.

"Are you working on something?"

"Sort of, but what about you?" Sarah asked, as if none of the visit had happened yet and they'd begun with chitchat after all. "I haven't even asked about your work. Your website is beautiful."

"Thanks; I need to update it." Kiki nodded to Sylvie on the floor. "I've been pretty neglectful."

Arman sat down in the club chair above Kiki. He put his hands on her shoulders. "You haven't been neglectful."

"Not with *Sylvie*." She balked. "My work."

"Oh."

"He barely realizes I have a business."

"Come on," Arman said lightly, "I do, too. I love her designs. You should have seen our place in L.A. . . . ."

"You know, I finally saw your second film," Kiki said.

"Why?" Sarah said. "It's terrible. I told you it was terrible."

"I didn't recognize it as yours." Kiki said to Matthew, "I didn't recognize her in it," as if this were something over which they might relate.

Matthew, smart man, didn't reply.

"Well," Sarah said, "it wasn't my script. You know that, right? I was hired to direct it."

"I just didn't feel you in it at all."

"Even if it's not your script, it's still your film," Arman added. "I mean, don't you think? Shouldn't it—theoretically at least— have your stamp?"

"Did you see it, too?" Sarah asked him.

"No. You asked us not to watch it. But theoretically—"

"Theoretically?"

"Sure, theoretically. *Theoretically*, it's your film."

"Okay," said Sarah. "Sure."

"It was just amazing to me that you directed it," said Kiki.

"So if you didn't see my *stamp* . . . is that a compliment be- cause it's such a bad film or . . ." Sarah let out a brittle laugh. "I can't tell."

"You know what," Matthew said carefully, "I think . . ."

Was he going to actually try answering not only for her but also for Kiki?

Then Sarah saw that Matthew looked distracted or maybe even worse, and she knew there was more going on. "I think," Matthew repeated slowly, "I—"

"You think *what*?"

Matthew looked right at Sarah, as if no one else were there. "I think I might have to go lie down."

"Oh?" She erupted into hollow laughter.

Matthew looked at her and then at Kiki and Arman. "I'm just suddenly really exhausted."

"Is this about before?" Sarah asked.

"Before?" Matthew's tone was somewhere between aggressive and genuinely confused.

"Yesterday. Because I'm going to," Sarah said quietly. "I told you I will."

"You guys," said Kiki uncomfortably, "maybe you want to take a walk or something?"

Arman stood up. "My God"—he looked at Kiki with naked exasperation—"you're so afraid of confrontation."

"Don't raise your voice," Kiki said.

"I'm not raising my voice. All I'm saying is, let them fight a little. Let them air their bullshit. We have ours. They have theirs. People don't always need to get along. Everything doesn't have to be okay. And they know that. They understand that. And that's why they'll be fine."

"Fine seems pretty relative."

"Fine *is* pretty relative."

Kiki stood and picked up Sylvie. "I'm going to put her down. I don't want her hearing all this."

"She's *eight months old*," cried Arman. "She's hearing noise."

"It's upsetting her. I can tell. She understands more than you think she does."

"I was raised in a house where no one ever spoke in a neutral tone of voice. Everyone yelled. Everyone yelled all the time!"

"Well, I don't love that paradigm. Sorry, it's not 1975."

And Kiki left the room with beloved and hard-won Sylvie Jane Simonian. *Bless her*, Sarah thought. *Please. Bless her and keep her safe.*

"She's not even tired," Arman hollered after Kiki. "Her sleeping is messed up enough as it is." They could hear Kiki's footsteps going up the stairs and padding across the hallway. "*What?*" he said to Sarah. "Don't give me that disapproving look. It *is*. She read this book about babies needing twice as much sleep as previously thought. Did you ever put your eight-month-old to sleep whenever she seemed remotely tired?"

"It doesn't matter what I did."

Matthew opened the door.

"Where are you going?" Sarah asked. "I thought you were exhausted."

He ignored her and stepped outside.

"Matthew," she called after him; the screen door slammed shut.

Arman was shaking his head, suppressing a grin.

"Don't shake your head at me," she said lightly, before realizing how insulted she was. "We aren't getting along. It's a little ugly. I know that."

"You know ugly?"

"I do."

"Real ugliness?"

"Yes," she said quietly, "I know about that, too."

"Why do I doubt that?"

"I don't know." She twisted her hands together, squeezed until her rings dug into her skin. "I can't help you there."

"You know, when we moved up here, I wasn't exactly prepared for the poverty. It's real."

"Of course it's real. This was news to you?"

"People are pissed."

"As they should be."

"People are really pissed. The factories are all closing, there's meth everywhere, and the heroin—"

"And what?" she asked, while getting a handle on his tone, which was increasingly condescending. "You identify with these people in crisis?"

"I do, actually."

"You do."

He nodded. "I mean, I get it. I get why they resent me and what I look like."

"And you look like what—a movie star?"

"Some guy wouldn't sell me firecrackers last month because he thought I was 'an Arab.'"

"Jesus. That's infuriating."

"I'm no movie star, Sarah. We both know that."

"Ah, *aha*. But you look like one." She smiled.

Arman shook his head with a laugh that seemed distinctly bittersweet. "They see me as an outsider and threatening."

"Mmm-hmm."

"They want to protect what they have. What little they have."

"We both know this story and how it ends. Every day there's a retelling of this story. Please don't tell me you're sympathetic to—what do they call it now?—racial resentment? Racial anxiety?"

"You don't have any idea. You just don't."

She was disturbed by where this conversation was headed, that he seemed hell-bent on exposing her privileged cluelessness, but she was also afraid of how angry Matthew was. He usually took a run or a walk to ward off rage and despair. She looked out the window. He was nowhere in sight. She kept thinking she should go find him, but she also knew that if she did, that if she tried to question him right then, he would leave her. Somehow she knew he would.

"I'm no fucking movie star. Why would you say that? *Why would you say that to me?* It's humiliating."

She turned and looked at Arman sitting on the couch. He put his head in his hands. It was eerie how much he looked the way he had outside in the middle of the night. She found herself wondering, *Do we all repeat the same gestures every day? If we stripped away the words, the weather, and the noise, would our days be nothing but repetitive choreography?*

The neighbor—he had seen her with Arman. He had stuck his fingers beneath her bathing suit and pulled. He had seen them talking outside and made an assumption.

Why had she pretended to be Kiki?

Why not? she answered herself immediately. *Why not be Kiki if the option presented itself? At least for an afternoon?*

Unable to commit to either standing or sitting, she leaned against the wall. "I'm sorry."

Arman shrugged it off. "It's okay."

"No, I'm really sorry." Though she hadn't exactly intended it, she recognized she was offering a larger, more all-encompassing apology, one for how she'd opted out of their lives. "I mean, I realize it's probably too late. I realize you probably don't give a shit."

He scratched his beard. "I do." His bluster was suddenly gone. "I do give a shit. Come here. Come sit down."

She walked over and sat on the other side of the couch.

"Look," he said.

"*What?*"

"I don't want to fight with you."

"You don't? You sort of seem to."

"I do?"

She nodded.

"Well, I don't know what to say. I'm sorry, too." Arman looked, for the first time, like . . . a dad. A worn-out dad on a Sunday.

"It's okay," she said. "Really, let's just stop."

He nodded and stretched his wrist out. He did a trick with his hands that made it look as if he'd cut off his thumb. He'd performed this trick years ago for Leda, who'd loved it and giggled, but Sarah had screamed so loudly that no one had ever let her forget it.

"Arman," she warned now. "Stop!"

He gave her a smile as if he was giving her a gift, but at least for the moment she *did* feel more relaxed.

"So, I know it wouldn't occur to Matthew," Arman said, in a weird sort of hurry, "but he shoots so many ads, so many, and even one national ad—just *one*—I mean, do you understand how much actors get paid for one ad—even the voice work? . . . It just—I—" Arman shook his head.

Sarah blinked, then blinked again; she needed to take out her contacts. She remembered being fitted for eyeglasses in the fifth grade. The case was blue. She wore them on the trip home. While sitting in the back seat of the car, she looked out the window. It was as if the world had suddenly announced itself in every leaf on every tree. She hadn't realized that one could actually *see the shapes of leaves*, that it was even possible from a distance. The ordinary view was crystalline suddenly and all too much. She remembered now the sound of her father's gravelly voice and the static on the radio; she remembered returning the glasses to their blue suede case. She'd closed her eyes for the rest of the trip. This, she realized, was how she felt just then.

"Sarah? Did you hear what I said?"

She nodded. "I'll be right back." Then she got up and walked upstairs.

Kiki was on the window seat, surrounded by books. She had enormous headphones on, plugged into her phone. From the way her whole body was vaguely grooving, Sarah imagined she was listening to music, but Kiki looked like that even when she was making a list of errands. For all Sarah knew Kiki could be tuning in to a political podcast, a Spanish lesson, white noise.

She registered Sarah standing there and didn't appear surprised. She took a moment before removing her headphones.

"Sylvie's sleeping?"

Kiki nodded. "She was exhausted."

"All that sun," Sarah said dumbly.

Kiki nodded, unplugging the headphones and wrapping the cord around and around until it was neat and secure.

"And all that tension," Sarah added. "Of course you're right about that. I'm sure she felt it."

Kiki nodded again.

"I'm sorry. And I'm sorry it's taken me this long to understand why you got in touch."

"What are you talking about?"

"I'm sorry. I understand now. I spoke to Arman and I get it."

"What are you talking about?"

"I guess I was so happy when you reached out that it didn't occur to me to think about why. I'd always wanted to contact you again, but it felt like the window had closed. I was just happy to hear from you. To be honest, I was exceptionally happy. It was overwhelming."

"What are you talking about? I told you why I finally got in touch. Because we had Sylvie."

Sarah shook her head.

"Leda was the first kid I'd ever really spent time with. *I loved her*. I loved being around the three of you. Even if it took me too long to understand this, being around you and Matt and Leda made me think differently about having a family. Why don't you seem to want to hear that?"

Sarah couldn't stop shaking her head.

"What are you thinking?"

Sarah turned from Kiki before any tears came. She bounded down the stairs and steeled herself. She knew Kiki was following her. When she reached the living room, Arman was gone.

Kiki stood beside her. "Where did he go?"

Through the screen came the scent of sun-blasted grass.

"Is that them?" Sarah pointed toward the footbridge, where two men were crossing.

"No. No way. Those guys are younger and better looking."

Sarah laughed. "You got in touch with us again because you need money. I'm just embarrassed I didn't put it together before now. I'm sorry I've been so dense. Arman shouldn't have had to ask."

Kiki's brow furrowed and her forehead creased, and for a

moment she did look her age. "You think that's the reason I invited you here?"

"It's weird but I don't mind. I just wish you'd been up-front about it."

"I *am* up-front about it. We need money. We're in serious debt. How much more up-front can I be? But that's not why I got in touch."

"No?"

"No."

"You're going to tell me that Matthew's success did not pass through your mind as you wrote that first e-mail?"

Kiki shook her head. "This is really insulting." She shook her head more vehemently and then stopped, looking confused, as if she'd somehow shaken off whatever she'd actually wanted to say. Then she looked out the window. "When you're desperate, you think about everything."

"Yeah. I know that."

"You do?"

Sarah nodded.

Kiki's gaze became assiduous, as if she was taking in the full meaning of what Sarah had implied. *Desperate?* She could almost see Kiki's brain at work. *What on earth did Sarah have to be desperate about?*

"So . . . ?" Sarah encouraged.

"So, yes, it *passed through my mind* that maybe Matt might be able to introduce Arman to some casting directors or at least offer some connections in order to break into voice-over work, which for some reason has always strangely eluded him. Don't you think he has a great voice? Distinctive?"

"He does. It's always reminded me of my father's. He did voice work. Do you remember?"

"Of course. Of course I remember. Look, I don't know, maybe I fantasized that you'd fall so in love with Sylvie that I'd ask you to be her godmother and you'd—I don't know"—Kiki pulled at her knotty hair—"*I don't know*—pay for her nursery school like in a fucking modern-day fairy tale. Would you judge me? Do you judge me for that fantasy?"

Sarah thought about it briefly. "No, I don't."

"Of course you do. And, anyway, it's all ruined now because I told you!"

Sarah started laughing. "I forgot how funny you are."

"That's because I'm not."

"But you always end up making me laugh."

The room was getting darker. Leda was probably not in this time zone, but somewhere, at some point this month, she sat in a room and watched the light drain out of it.

"Where are they?" Sarah asked.

Kiki shrugged.

Sylvie let out a brief cry but then quieted immediately.

How tense Kiki had looked at the notion of Sylvie's waking up, how tense and genuinely frightened. Being a mother, Sarah reflected, was all too often like starring in a horror film. Then the screen door screeched open, and Kiki hissed, "Shh," at Matthew, then Arman behind him.

Matthew nodded. He stood up straight and cracked his neck. "Okay," he said to Sarah. "Let's move on. It's over."

Sarah went to him, put her hand in his. He didn't shake it off.

"Um," asked Kiki, "what's over?"

"Our fight," Sarah explained. She gave Matthew's hand a squeeze.

"Okay, good." Kiki brightened. "So, before I lose my nerve— Matt, I'm going to ask you a favor. Okay?" Her hands were balled into fists, Sarah noticed, as if someone had told her to stop talking with her hands. "Arman, I'm asking."

Sarah looked at Matthew hopefully but he didn't meet her eye.

"We're all right," Sarah whispered to Matthew. "We are."

"I can't believe you," Arman addressed Kiki heatedly. "I cannot believe you are doing this."

This seemed only to embolden her. "Arman went into the city yesterday not to shoot a film but because he couldn't deal with seeing you. He called me from his cell phone at four or five this morning, too stressed to come inside the house because he didn't want to reveal any of this to you and he was afraid that he would."

"Reveal what?" Matthew asked.

"That's who you were talking to," Sarah said, genuinely relieved that Arman wasn't cheating on Kiki.

Arman walked outside, the door banging shut behind him.

Kiki continued as if she barely noticed. "He thought he'd crack and let you know what's going on with us, how deep in the hole we are, and he's too proud to admit any of it. He was so angry that I invited you here." Her face twisted up into a painful grin.

"Why did you tell us he was on a film set?" Sarah asked.

"Have you *never* told a lie?"

"What's that supposed to mean?"

"It means give us a break," Kiki said. "I'm asking you to understand. Maybe you can't, but—"

"No," Sarah said, "of course I can."

"How much money do you need?" Matthew asked.

"I want to be clear," Kiki said. "That's not why you're here."

"Okay," Matthew said.

"That isn't why I got back in touch."

"I don't care," he said. "Just tell me."

Sarah found herself opening the screen door, careful to avoid the screech and slam. She looked outside and found that Arman was standing down by the water, across from the flag. She thought about going down to get him, but remembered what he said about being raised in a house of yelling. "Arman," she called out, "come back here."

When he didn't respond, she went back inside. Matthew was listening to Kiki, hushed and solemn. She was explaining the IVF, the insurance, and the debt.

"You did the right thing," Sarah interrupted, sounding angry and impatient. "Stop beating yourself up about it."

"You don't understand," Kiki muttered.

"We're going to help you." Sarah asked Matthew, "Right? All right?"

He nodded.

"So we'll help you. You'll figure it out. Just—*please*," Sarah begged, then again, "please."

"Please *what*?" Kiki asked. "*What*?"

Sarah thought of the tent in the woods; she thought of the man in the tent. He'd leaned her against a tree and she'd walked away unharmed. She'd courted danger and avoided it. It had made her feel better.

"Please stop wasting time."

MONDAY

HEN SARAH WAS A CHILD, HER FATHER gave her a password. She was to use it even if he knocked on their door and she asked *Who is it?* and it was her father saying *It's your father*; she was to ask for the password with her half of the password, and if he didn't respond with his half of the password, she was to never, not under any circumstance, let him in. Not even if they heard each other's voice, he'd explained, were they to let each other in. When they traveled, he never allowed anyone to put their home address on their luggage tags, in case the baggage handlers saw the tags and decided to go rob their empty house. He didn't believe in having food delivered, because what kind of person has a job delivering food? Do you want that person at your doorstep, getting a good look inside?

Whenever Sarah mentioned these . . . quirks, people inevitably asked, tentatively, if her mother had died by the hands of a criminal or if her father might have been a spy or involved in organized crime, and when Sarah responded that her mother hadn't (congenital heart defect when Sarah was nineteen months old) and that he wasn't (fluky and lucrative stint as the voice of Wrangler Denim, but a chemist, then a science teacher), all of these precautions seemed immediately and entirely crazy.

She thought of her father that night as she lay in bed after Sunday's dinner and too much wine. There had been a time—when she'd gotten pregnant young with Leda by accident—that being her father's daughter had served her. Before Leda, she'd been living a nocturnal, artistic, selfish life, subsisting on candy and bagels. But when she and Matthew decided to keep the baby, her days began and ended with the sun; she ate sweet potatoes, spinach, and yogurt. Soon after giving birth, she found herself sitting in the back of a local café with a group of exhausted women at least a decade her senior, each with a baby strapped to her body. She listened while they talked about feeding and sleeping; she shared her specific, now-long-forgotten fears and questions, and everyone looked ravaged and terrified. And in that moment she most understood her father. Sarah's mother died when Sarah was a baby. There was nothing her father could have done. And yet . . . *and yet.* She unfailingly described him as paranoid and would regularly recount his vigilant antics with wry, superior laughter, but while sitting in that café, she secretly began to believe that his ideas were not only sane but wise. So much of life is beyond our control. Shouldn't we be doing everything we possibly can to stay safe? To keep on living?

Everyone was so vulnerable. You were a fool ever to relax.

Of course by that point her father was dead.

And then the playing and the homework and the meals and the friends and the going to other kids' houses and the ordering socks and filling out forms and forgetting the bags and the checking where Leda was and the checking in and *just checking in!* The checking and checking and checking—through it all, she'd deferred to her father's voice.

But now?

She thought of her father now, wondering if even he'd agree that maybe it was time for her to stop doing all she possibly could. That maybe—at least for Sarah—such vigilance was useless? Would she and Matthew go right to the edge of hope every time they received calls from an unknown number? She hoped so. She didn't want to ever give up the anticipation. But it unnerved them every time.

Nothing she could do; this was all too clear. The phone calls and the waiting and the daily mental exertions—this had the same effect as doing nothing. She could ease up. She could let go. There were ways to learn. And there was freedom in that; wasn't there?

She went to the pink bathroom and drank water straight from the tap, pressed her fingers to her eyelids, and walked down the stairs.

Outside, under the stars dimmed by streetlights from town, in a yard she knew she'd envision over years to come, she stood and looked around. It was a lazy place, this place, but she didn't feel lazy. Everything felt heightened, as if she were being watched, which, yes, she might be. He'd seen her. He'd been watching.

Maybe right that second her phone, long gone, could be ringing and ringing and ringing and ringing with the Chime ringtone, which might as well have been called Contemporary Despair. Or any moment Leda could simply reappear. She could skip the phone call and already be lying in the hammock; Leda might be watching. The air was still, and then—as if Sarah had willed it, like those string lights last night—a gust of wind came and went. The wind was warm and reminded her of Florida, five years old and alone with her father. She remembered saying, *The air is so human*, again and again. She'd said it for days before he'd pointed out that what she meant to say was *humid. The air is humid. The air is human.*

There was a human. He was there. She noticed that after the wind died down the hammock kept moving. She knew it was Arman, but for a moment she let it be Leda. And there she was, right there, several yards away. Sarah could actually see—could she?—the blond hair spilling over the edge and down toward the earth, down into the darkness. There was the fungal stench of a girl who'd been riding a bus all night long. Sarah would approach quietly. She would wordlessly climb into the hammock and Leda would be startled. Leda would probably scream. It would be awkward at first, of course it would. But then they'd lie side by side as they always had—shoulders, arms, and thighs touching together—and eventually fall asleep.

Sarah put her fingers to her eyelids and pressed. She opened her eyes and crept toward the trees. As she grew closer, the blond hair spilling over the edge became dried-out overgrown weeds. The hammock continued to sway and her heart continued its beat and she knew she should speak up, that she could literally give Arman a heart attack (none of them—not even Arman and Kiki!—were young anymore), but somehow Sarah just couldn't. She couldn't call out. She stood several feet from where his head would be. He would lie facing the creek, not the house.

"Arman," she finally said. Her voice was faint at first, even hoarse. When he didn't pop up, she said it louder. Still he didn't move.

Why didn't she turn around and go back inside? Why didn't she take his silence as a clear message to leave him alone? She came closer. The parched tall weeds didn't sway. Nothing moved. She reached for the hammock and gripped the edge. Without intending to, without making a choice, she touched his thick hair. She heard him shift, obviously startled, but he didn't cry out or speak. It was dark, she was fumbling, she hadn't made any decision, but there she was with her hand on Arman's head. She kept it there, her hand, as if it were separate from her— maybe a bug that had landed and trapped itself. She waited for the bug to make its way out. She watched the creek and waited.

"I was waiting for you," he said.

When she realized it wasn't Arman, she retracted her

hand but didn't scream. "I thought you were my husband." She worked to catch her breath.

"No, you didn't."

He didn't rise from the hammock.

"What are you doing here?" she whispered.

"I'm here to talk to you."

"You need to leave."

He didn't move from his spot in the hammock. "You don't mean that."

"I do." Sarah glanced back at the house. "Yes, I do."

"Nah."

She wondered if he was drunk. "You don't belong here." She checked across the creek. Were there more people? The house was dark. Was that even his house? "You don't belong here and you need to leave."

He went to sit up, not without struggle, wincing as if from an old injury.

She moved away from the hammock, looked back at the house again. Her heart plunged into her stomach; she could swear someone was sitting at the outdoor table now.

"I don't belong here," he acknowledged.

"Listen, I'm married and you need to get out of here."

"Right," he said, more quietly now. "Got it."

She turned and nervously retreated toward the house, praying he wouldn't follow. She made it as far as the outdoor table and she was right, she hadn't hallucinated, there was Arman, outside again, with his head resting on his arms. He hadn't been sitting there when she came outside mere minutes ago. Had he followed close behind, saying nothing? Now he looked as if he might even be asleep, but he raised his head and squinted, as if to place her. She should have told him a stranger was in the hammock, a stranger that—if he was to be believed—lived in the house across the creek. *Be careful*, she should have said. But what two words were more useless?

"Who were you talking to?" Arman asked.

"Me," the man said, and he was suddenly there and Arman was on his feet and they were all standing around the table.

"What the hell?" Arman yelled. "Wait—we talked about the telephone wire. You live over there." Arman recovered slightly or was at least making an effort to appear more at ease.

The man nodded. "We were talking," he said calmly. "Her and I were talking." She could feel the weight of him standing next to her. His voice was deep, congested.

"What is going on here? What are you doing in our yard?" Arman asked sort of lightly, as if maybe he were dreaming or overreacting and this strange middle-of-the-night convergence could still turn out to be a neighborly misunderstanding.

"You know what?" asked the man. "People do nothing. People talk a big fucking game about being citizens, being brave, but then? What?" He made a show of looking around. "Fuckin' crickets."

"Listen, man," said Arman, "I'm not sure what your problem is, but it's the middle of the night and you're on my property."

"Ain't your property. You're renting. You came up here and—day one—I knew something was messed up. When you asked me about that phone wire, you should've seen your face.

As if you have any right whatsoever to be so goddamn demand-ing. I mean, it's you who doesn't belong here. It's you who doesn't belong. Do you understand what I'm saying to you?"

Sarah said, "Listen—"

"Do you?"

"I've already heard this," said Arman, "so you can spare me. I've heard it all before."

Well, Sarah thought, *so much for sympathy toward racial resentment.*

Arman put his hands in the air as if to surrender, as if he'd do anything not to strike this guy but that he was getting close.

"I told you," Sarah told the man. "You need to leave. *Right now.*"

He came around the table. He moved quickly, surprisingly so, and before Sarah even registered what was coming, he leaned into Arman and said, "You disgust me."

"Get the fuck out of here, I mean it."

"If you do anything to him," Sarah warned the man, "you'll be charged with a hate crime. Do you get that? Do you? 'You disgust me.' What is wrong with you?"

"*Hate crime?* You've got to be fucking kidding me. He can't just beat you."

"Excuse me?" balked Arman.

"*What?!*" Sarah cried. She was starting to shake with impa-tience.

"He hits you." The man pointed at Arman. "I know some-thing like that? I don't stand by."

"This is unbelievable," said Arman.

"*What are you talking about?*" cried Sarah, then she finally understood:

Who're you hiding from?

My husband.

"Just get off my property," said Arman.

Now Matthew was slamming the screen door and running outside, and Kiki was right behind him, taking photos of the man with her phone.

"You'd better leave," Matthew told him.

"She told me you hit her," he said to Arman, sounding—for the first time—unsteady.

Neighbors' lights were coming on. Soon, the cops might arrive.

"Why would I say that?" countered Sarah. "Apologize to him."

"You want me to apologize to your husband."

"That's not my husband."

"But—"

"This is my husband." She took Matthew's arm.

"Ah, I get it." The man pointed to Matthew. "You. You are seriously fucked."

Matthew only said, "Get out of here."

"And burn your flag," Sarah said. "That flag makes me sick."

"My grandfather gave me that flag."

"Oh, I'm sure he did."

"It's Russian navy. You think this is the first time I heard this ignorant shit? It's a similar design but it's not a Confederate flag and I'm not taking it down. I'm no racist." The man cast a glance at each of them and landed on Sarah. "I came here—Jesus—I wanted to protect you."

"To protect me?" She looked straight into the man's eyes, which were light and strange, with flat dark lashes and a thick brow. She stood up taller and didn't look away. "No."

"Sarah," Matthew demanded. "You need to tell us what's going on."

In the dark, looking so lost, she could imagine him older—no, *old*: exposed scalp and loose skin and memory fully shot.

"I met him today," she said matter-of-factly. She knew enough to know she couldn't afford to appear sheepish. "We met in the woods while you were swimming."

"Right," Matthew said. "Of course you did."

"He must have seen my cut and bruises and . . . I don't know."

"You don't know?"

The man muttered something, then walked away. They stopped their arguing to watch him. Just like that: he made his way toward the street—gone.

Kiki and Arman went inside.

"I was upset," Sarah finally said, turning her attention from Kiki and Arman to Matthew. "I was really upset. I think the mugging . . . Look, with that guy—I was evasive."

"Did you lie?"

"I may have." She nodded. "Sometimes I feel like lying to everyone about everything."

The man appeared on the footbridge and they watched him slowly cross it. He entered the dark house and turned on a light.

"Do you never have that impulse?" she asked.

Matthew looked up at the burned-out-negative clouds before finally shaking his head. "What I think of as my life—I think it's over."

She nodded.

"So I guess," Matthew continued, "I'd like a new one. A new life."

"Without me." Dawn was coming. Violets and browns were outpacing the darkness; she wasn't ready.

"Not you like this."

She nodded, feeling calmer than she had any right to. "I've never thought of myself as someone who blows it all up."

"I've never thought of you like that either. But . . . people change."

She swallowed, hard. Would he actually leave? She thought of the man on the subway.

Do you think people ever really change? The orange-pink light. The dark glow of the underground.

"What?" Matthew asked, abruptly gripping her shoulders. She didn't flinch. "Do you disagree?" He dug his fingers deeper. "Do you not see how much you've changed?" When he began to shake her, it was hard.

She felt her chest heaving up and down; it was as if her internal organs were jockeying for position.

"Harder," she said.

He let go.

"I mean it. Please."

"Sometimes"—he sat down at the table—"I don't really know if the person I knew—the one who made, you know, *films*, but also made meals and appointments and who just generally got shit done with a lot of energy and was really dynamic and—you know, *that person*—did I invent her?" He stood up again, looked at her straight on. "Was that you? I mean, it had to be you, right? You did all those things. You were also just . . . lovely." He grinned the most miserable grin. "You were thoughtful and you were fun."

"I was not."

"You really were. I mean, at least most of the time."

She moved closer, lightly touched his shoulder. It was as if, for a moment, they were at a crowded party and he was simply someone she knew.

"We should check on them." He nodded to the house.

"I'm sure they're fine."

"But still."

"No, of course." She rose to her feet and started to follow him. They had once sat in the shade of an oak tree in Madison, Wisconsin. He'd cracked all his knuckles and sheepishly smiled.

"I met someone on a subway recently," she said. "It was a strange conversation."

He turned back to face her, looking down the slight incline. "A man, I'm guessing."

She shook her head. "I mean, yes, a man, but old."

"Right, okay. And?"

"I think we should hire another investigator."

"Honey," he sighed.

"I don't want to give up."

"I know."

Then he resumed walking toward the house.

She stayed outside alone, and just like that, dawn was turning to morning. The same leathery skinny woman that she'd seen the other day—the one smoking, pushing a baby carriage full of groceries—she was crossing the footbridge toward town. Still smoking, still pushing that carriage, but this time it was empty.

INSIDE, ARMAN WAS making a pot of coffee. "So," he said flatly, "we're really tired. I think you should maybe head out after breakfast." Then he cleared his throat and looked at them as if they were stragglers at a party that had ended several hours before.

"Of course," Sarah said.

They headed upstairs to collect their things. She realized that, astonishingly, Sylvie was still sleeping. Midway up the stairs, she looked down and saw Arman and Kiki locked in obvious disagreement. She followed Matthew into the bedroom and silently gathered their belongings. Matthew stood in the middle of the room, opening and closing his hands as if they'd fallen asleep. On the way downstairs, Sarah abruptly sat on a step and Matthew joined her. She buried her face in his shoulder.

Their duffel bags tumbled down the staircase.

"What happened?" cried Kiki.

"It's okay." Matthew sounded as if he were broken and his voice could no longer hide this fact.

Arman picked up the duffels and brought them to the threshold. He dropped the bags but stood there, as if he was considering opening the door and heading out himself.

Kiki walked over and looked up at Sarah and Matthew.

Kiki sat on the bottom step, facing the front door. It seemed as though she might go talk to Arman. But when she finally spoke, it was quietly and it wasn't to him. "Are you going to tell me what's going on with Leda?"

"She's a drug addict," Sarah said to the back of Kiki's head. "Heroin."

Kiki looked up to face them and burst into tears. She put her face in her hands. From their vantage they could see, under the gray cotton garment that she'd barely removed all weekend that somehow worked equally well as a nightgown or party dress—the rise and fall of Kiki's narrow back.

"It's okay," said Matthew, though *it was not it was not it was not*. "She's sober now."

"Fuck," said Arman, coming over and leaning on the balustrade. "*Fuck*. But she's okay?"

"She cut off contact with us," said Sarah, her eyes fixed on the tar-black-painted stairs.

In the lobby of a Scottsdale hotel she'd recognized a fellow visitor to the rehab facility. They'd given each other weary smiles and started talking. The woman was young and slight. She wore a delicate heart necklace. Her ex-marine husband had gotten hooked after returning from Afghanistan. *It's lucky your daughter never started in with the black tar.*

The words *lucky. Black tar.*

"But," asked Kiki, "her birthday? And the boat?"

She had to know the answer by the silence that followed. She'd wanted the missing piece and now she had it.

"Four years ago," Sarah finally said, "after she'd been sober for a little more than a year, she left on a yoga retreat. When she didn't return our calls or e-mails, we hired a private investigator, who eventually figured out that the yoga retreat was connected to some kind of empowerment project in Pasadena, run by a couple who'd been investigated by the FBI years before when they'd run a similar program in Florida."

"Are you serious?" asked Arman. Sarah thought he might kick the newel. "She's in a cult?"

"She packed up her purple duffel bag and flew to L.A., and I thought, 'How great is that? How great is it that she's taking such good care of herself?' Remember?" Sarah asked Matthew, with the kind of bitter laughter she hated most about herself.

Without any internal warnings, Sarah suddenly needed to move. She stood, walked quickly down the stairs as if she were rushing somewhere specific. She went into the kitchen, filled a glass with water even though she wasn't thirsty. When she came into the living room, they were all waiting. "At first, when I heard she was in this group, I thought, 'Okay,'" she continued, as if there'd been no interruption. "I thought, 'Sure, fine. So she may be a bit addicted to yoga and she might need to follow some kind of strict health regime,' but I wasn't about to start in about how any addiction was an addiction. If we had a yoga-addicted, maybe vegan, maybe-a-little-too-earnest daughter? If she lived a clean and sober life? You would never hear me complain. You'd never hear me make one stupid joke. Never."

"Of course," said Kiki. "But how—"

"At the time, when we found out that the group's head-quarters was in Pasadena, I thought, 'Well, Matthew travels so much for work that it doesn't really matter where we live,' so I found a rental in Pasadena. Then I tried, almost every day for weeks, to talk to Leda, but it became very clear that she was discouraged from speaking with us. When I did see her, I tried to say anything I possibly could to get her away. This accomplished nothing except that she distanced herself further. At some point I tried to step back and really understand what she was doing, and when I asked the most basic questions, she responded that the integrity of the group's intellectual property was so important that in order to protect their trade secrets, which had been, you know, developed at great time and expense, she wasn't allowed to talk about anything. She actually said—with a completely straight face—that she wasn't allowed to disclose the group's proprietary methods and materials. So then Matthew hired a very expensive deprogrammer, who couldn't even get Leda to talk to him, which led to Matthew not coming back to Pasadena."

"That's not true," Matthew said quietly.

"It is. It is." Sarah remembered his saying Leda was no longer a child. That she was sober now and it was her life, her choice. She remembered this because she remembered thinking but not saying that maybe he was right. "It *is* true."

Matthew continued to shake his head.

"It doesn't matter," Sarah said. "She moved with the group farther south, then across the border and off the grid, and then she completely cut off contact."

"At least you saw her again," said Matthew.

"It's true. I did. I saw her once, over a year ago. Matthew and I had just gotten back together. He was across the world when she called home and said she was ready for a visit. I flew to where she was then—who knows where she is now, we can't find her anymore—and she said she wanted to tell us in person that we needed to let her go. That she was healthier and happier not being in touch with family. She said she harbored neither anger nor ill will. She wanted us to see just how well she was doing. It all sounded as if she'd been given a script."

"I'm so sorry," Kiki said.

"By the time I flew down there, only a week or so later, the whole operation was gone," Matthew said. "They must have picked up and left right after Sarah did. No one in the town around there knew who I was talking about. It was like they'd never been there."

"Jesus," said Arman. "Jesus."

"These days"—Sarah swirled ice in her glass—"here's what I think with some frequency: 'Fuck yoga.' Just, seriously? 'Fuck yoga.' Isn't that stupid?"

Matthew picked up their bags.

"But you can't go *now*," Kiki cried. "Please don't go."

Sarah felt a smile coming on, cracking her face wide open. "'Please don't go,'" she repeated, and felt the smile in her chest, her toes. "'We'll eat you up—we love you so.'"

"What?" Arman asked, baffled, mirroring her smile.

"Maurice Sendak," said Matthew. "*Where the Wild Things Are.*"

Kiki and Arman stared back at them, uncomprehending. They hadn't yet spent hours and hours reading books to their child, hadn't watched that child relish the repetition of her favorites. They didn't yet have boxes of children's books with which they couldn't bear to part. They had it all ahead of them.

"I'm sorry I lied," said Sarah. "I'm so sorry. I'm sorry about your neighbor and about—" She shook her head, unable to continue, and reached for Kiki's hands. Sarah pulled Kiki into a hug, trying and failing to catch her breath. She was taller than Kiki but Kiki's arms were longer, and she wrapped those pale arms around Sarah, holding her tight. They stayed there together and Kiki smelled like flowers and powder and slightly sour milk. Sarah let her vision blur and didn't worry about how she was wetting Kiki's perfect, chic pajama dress with stupid, pointless tears. How could a person cry so much? She supposed it was similar to eating and drinking and sex; it felt novel every time.

Sarah finally pulled away. "You were my best friend, too." When Kiki laughed, Sarah didn't. "Did you think I was going to leave without saying that?"

"I did, actually."

"Well, you were wrong, all wrong."

Matthew put his hand on Arman's shoulder and told them, "I'll be in touch. Please don't worry."

When Leda had done her first cartwheel on that deserted beach in Baja, the sun had blinded Sarah as her daughter flipped upside down. During the second cartwheel, Sarah felt one moment of pure relief when Leda's pink T-shirt fell over her head and revealed not only a cute yellow bikini top and a fleshier but still-thin belly but also no more belly-button piercing. In that moment of dumb relief that her daughter no longer had a belly piercing, Sarah came closer. She couldn't take her eyes off Leda: young, lovely, no longer sick with addiction. Then she caught her breath.

Sweetheart, what is that?

Leda was out of breath, smiling. *What is what?*

Did you get burned?

Leda's expression changed. She held down the hem of her threadbare shirt. *Why are you scrutinizing me?*

I'm not. Did you get burned?

No.

Above your hip?

No.

Is it a tattoo?

No.

Let me see it.

Why? You're being creepy.

Sarah came closer. Behind her daughter, the crashing waves. The nearly blinding sunshine. Leda lifted her shirt with an extravagant gesture. Whether she was being defiant or carefree was impossible to tell.

A square of raised pink skin, a small square, looked—on closer inspection—like two snakes or maybe someone's initials.

She'd been branded.

SARAH LOOKED OUT the window of the moving car. She remembered again the day she got glasses. A child with a blue suede case. *Don't worry*, Matthew had said to Kiki and Arman. It was what he always said. She'd taken off the glasses. She'd returned them to their case.

She wondered what had happened to that woman by the lakeshore. Would she ever learn to swim?

Should Sarah have confronted the man? Told him to stop? To stop what? *Teasing?*

Outside: the trees, their blurry green leaves, the endless nothing sky.

There were so many things they didn't talk about anymore.

seven

MONDAY EVENING

I'LL MAKE DINNER," SHE SAID.

He shook his head. "We're out of everything."

"I'll shop. It's not that late. I'd really like to cook."

"I just—"

"Unless you're starving." *Please don't leave me.* "Are you starving?"

"I'm not starving."

"Can I have the new house keys?"

He looked at her blankly.

"You changed the locks. I forgot to take a set."

"Oh, right, of course." He fished around in his pockets and took out a key ring.

They'd come home from the country earlier in the day. Matthew had napped, but then Sarah insisted they get back outside. They'd walked over the Brooklyn Bridge and into Chinatown and back. They'd bought cheap sunglasses and hadn't said much. And even though their walk had been at least three hours, he said, "I think I'll keep walking."

His expression still held a trace of what she'd seen when he'd stood on Kiki and Arman's lawn, looking confused and suddenly old. "You were right." He removed a set of keys and handed them over. "It felt good to get out."

As Sarah took the keys from him, as she climbed the stoop and gave him a forced, cheerful wave, she had the odd thought that there'd been no mugging after all, only her own stupidity. That instead of being held up at gunpoint a couple of nights ago, she'd mistakenly thrown her keys instead of an apple core out the car window, or maybe she forgot them in a rest stop along I-95.

As she turned the key in the lock, she heard the much-contested landline ringing. Matthew would have liked to yank it out of the wall long ago. He argued that each time it was a telemarketer and not Leda, it was another form of torture. Even after opting out and entering their number onto every make-it-stop list, the telemarketers didn't stop; they would never stop. So, Matthew argued, the landline had to go. But Sarah had prevailed—Leda knew the number by heart, they'd managed to keep the same number through several residences—and the phone was ringing right now in their kitchen, and Sarah's heart raced with magical thinking as she ran through the house.

After Sarah's frantic and repeated "Hello," whoever was on the line hesitated and then hung up. The caller ID said this was a blocked number. *Thanks for that useful tidbit, caller ID! Thanks so very fucking much!* She slammed down the phone. The lights were off. Given they didn't have central air, the house was remarkably cool. She picked up the receiver and took a breath. *Hello*, she practiced in her head, before saying it aloud. When she was growing up, other kids were trained to say their families' names when they answered the phone—*Zamora residence, Coleman residence*—but not Sarah. She'd been instructed to never give her name or her father's name to anyone who called. She usually tried not to think about her father and how her daily decisions—giving a stranger on the subway her home address right before taking a trip, for instance—might strike him. She tried with considerable success not to think of him and his suspicious worldview and how much he would have adored and been broken by Leda, but she thought of him right then with curious longing as the phone rang again.

When she heard her name, she was so startled that she flung her hand and knocked a glass off the counter. With her head cradling the phone to her shoulder, she turned on the lights and took the broom from the closet.

"Good evening, this is Officer Macavinta of the NYPD."

She expected Officer Macavinta to say Leda's name, but Sarah kept hearing her own name instead.

She heard a list of items that all belonged to her.

"And no phone?" she confirmed. She had to turn it into a question, as if asking might change the answer. "Got it. I'm coming." But after hanging up, she just stood there—broom in hand—looking at the glittering floor.

Long before three nights ago, when they'd filed the report, they'd been familiar with their precinct. Before Leda was arrested for possession of marijuana and heroin as a high school senior, she'd been given a warning as a sophomore for smoking pot, basically right in front of the precinct, with two friends. Such an event now seemed quaint. Starting in sixth grade, she'd gone to a well-regarded private school, famous for not giving grades and valuing the arts at least as highly as mathematics. The two friends had also gone to this school, had done the same escalating drugs right along with Leda on the same timeline, but one was currently getting a Ph.D. in evolutionary biology at Cornell, and the other was the front man of a band whose second album had recently been reviewed in *The New Yorker*. According to several profiles, this musician friend (who'd loved Sarah's tuna, lemon, and basil pasta and always forgot his hat, his keys, and his homework folders at their house) was living outside Nashville on a modest farm with a lovely looking girl-friend and hadn't used drugs since his "messed-up teenaged years."

How had these friends moved past those years unscathed? How were they healthy and successful while Leda had done little since that arrest aside from suffer?

It had occurred to Sarah that Leda was no longer suffering, and that maybe she had the ability to discard whatever didn't serve her, and in this case what didn't serve her was her parents. *You mean*, Matthew asked, when Sarah had mentioned this idea, *like a sociopath?*

Leda had been able to braid hair so elaborately that in high school she started charging for it. She ate frozen waffles out of the freezer, claiming they tasted better that way. She would dive off any rock, cliff, or board without hesitation. When she shaved off her long hair, when she went swimming in the icy Atlantic in December on a dare, when she stood up to a teacher who accused her of cheating, Sarah and Matthew had thought she was brave. And she was brave, no question. Leda was brave. Even after she became addicted to heroin. Maybe especially then. The things she did. The places she went. When Sarah said this at Family Day during one of the several excruciating Family Days Matthew and she went to—Florida, Arizona—people acted as if she were Susan Sontag saying the men who flew planes into the World Trade Center weren't cowards.

Sarah ascended the stairs of the precinct, repeated the same information to several people, signed papers, and accepted her bag. Everything but her wallet and phone was still inside: now-useless keys, hardcover book, lip gloss, Advil, tampon, coral lip and cheek tint, even the pamphlet about scheduling a mammogram that she'd been using as a bookmark.

She said thank you.

She walked out.

The longer she walked, the farther away she had to hold the bag. It may as well have transformed into a live serpent right there in her hand. She remembered a friend coming back from Japan and marveling at the beauty of that country, the citizens' pride, how efficiently life unfolded. According to this friend, there weren't public garbage cans, as it wouldn't have occurred to anyone to discard their waste in public. *How wonderful*, Sarah had agreed, but secretly she'd thought, *How oppressive*. How terrible to feel so constantly responsible. How unfailingly small and tidy and good could a person possibly be? She was glad for the wire can on the street corner. She dropped in her bag with all of its contents and kept walking.

Hi, Leda had said during the last phone call, the one that had brought Sarah to Baja. *It's me.*

Please, please. Please just tell me where you are.

She'd expected Leda's refusal, just as she'd expected some tears. But there were neither. Leda said she was sorry for causing any pain. She said she was ready for a visit. Sarah took down the information and was on a plane to Baja the next day.

Now it was almost nighttime. She'd planned to buy groceries on her way home from the precinct, but as she left, she thought, why not go a bit out of the way to the much-better market where she could buy fresher produce and still get home with enough time to cook? Sarah would make a simple and healthy and virtuous dinner, a meal to recharge and revive. Also, the bar (or restaurant) owned by the son of the old man from the subway was on a street near the much-better market. This was not why she was going there; Sarah would not be stopping for a drink at St. Ivo on her way home, though nothing would have been wrong with that. When Leda was in elementary school, Sarah had a mom-friend who had one drink by herself every day before coming home from work, and she seemed like one of the sanest people Sarah had ever known. And what would it hurt to take a look at the place? To see if St. Ivo did serve food and if the old man had been telling the truth about his son being the owner? She had no reason to think he'd been lying, but she couldn't stop thinking about her father. *Let's say you go to a restaurant. Let's say you order the fish. Unless that fish comes out with a head and tail, unless it's a distinct fish, one that you're familiar with—let's say salmon—that fish can be anything. You think you know what fish you're eating? You don't know.*

She and Matthew only ever went to the same four restaurants; they needed small changes, different places. She decided now that she had to give each day more effort. She could call this research and return with Matthew some other night if the place was appealing. He worked hard; she forgot that most of the time.

You are a good mother.

The man on the train had said this. She was sure of it. She knew it was silly but this was the only reason she had to go to this bar, why she had no choice but to at least try to see him again.

There was an alley to the side of the building, unusual for the neighborhood. She saw a man stacking trays of glassware. She watched as he stacked, as the glasses piled up. Sarah wasn't sure why she watched him, but she told herself she'd walk away after the last tray.

But then he finished. He checked his phone, he pressed his fingers to his temples, and there she still was, motionless. He went inside the bar through the side door. Almost immediately, he came back out again, this time with the old man from the subway. It was so strange to see him again; it was just as surprising as it would have been to discover that she'd imagined him. The two men were speaking low, in Czech, which she was familiar enough with to recognize but not to understand. Also, they had an urgency, or maybe it only seemed that way because what was she doing there, watching? The old man looked different—more gruff?—his movements were quicker; he hastily lit a cigarette and the younger man waved the smoke away.

If she'd had a phone, she knew it would be dinging with a text from Matthew right about then, that he wanted to go ahead and order in, that it was getting late. If she'd had a phone, she would have felt compelled to text Kiki and Arman, thanking them, apologizing, thanking them again. Sarah knew she was much warmer over texts and e-mails than in person. But since she had no phone, Kiki and Arman were spared her compulsive apologizing, and Matthew had no way of reaching her. There were no texts, no calls. There was nothing but time going by, the slight twinge of hunger pangs.

She went to the classical-music-playing market, bizarrely determined to make dinner for Matthew, even though he would happily have eaten cereal or a take-out burrito. She bought mahi-mahi and bok choy and avocado. She bought cardamom ice cream. While she speed-walked home, leaves blazed green under streetlights; flyers stapled to telephone poles curled up at their fraying edges.

YOU'RE ALLOWED TO COME HERE? she'd asked Leda on that deserted beach, after teasing her about the cartwheels.

Allowed? I'm not trapped. We've gone over this.

You know what I mean.

Come on, Leda said. *Let's walk.*

How many miles is it?

Who knows.

Leda had had her teeth fixed, Sarah noticed. They looked a little too white but it was still a vast improvement. Sarah wondered if the group had paid for it. Maybe it was one of the ways they'd lured her. Sarah and Matthew had offered to get her teeth fixed after she'd been sober for a year, but Leda had decided to go to L.A. instead. How Leda's teeth had looked when they'd found her that last time before she'd gotten clean: as though her mother had not made appointments and kept them; as though a mother had not diligently taken her daughter to a dentist and orthodontist until the daughter's nearly perfect teeth were actually perfect, not so long ago. Leda, age thirteen, had terrible canker sores along her bottom lip; the sores were so bad that she'd cried daily. When Sarah asked the orthodontist what could be done, the orthodontist recommended that Leda toughen up, and Sarah lit into the orthodontist amid a waiting room full of people. She yelled, *My daughter is in pain. Do you hear me? My daughter is in tremendous pain.*

SHE PREHEATED THE OVEN and became inexplicably thirsty. Had those painkillers been the beginning? Sarah hated that question. She had asked it too many times to count. She had been told by myriad professionals that, no, she did not cause her daughter's addiction. She could recall that orthodontist's waiting room perfectly, though, and the recollection made her feel slightly sick. She gulped down water, prepared the fish, began sautéing bok choy. She scanned her memory for every conceivable point of contact, though none of them had been fruitful for at least two years. Her top three numbers: landline of a house out in Rockaway where Leda had lived with a boyfriend (and his senile grandmother) after barely graduating from high school; cell phone of the cold and intelligent sponsor from the first stint in rehab; cell phone of the roommate during the brief golden era following the second stint in rehab. Sarah had even met this roommate; she'd helped Leda move into the Ditmas Park apartment as if they were any normal mother and daughter. The day had been especially windy, and when Sarah had left the apartment and was nearly swept sideways, she remembered thinking how the weather itself was resetting the course of their lives, shoving pain and despair into the gutter along with the trampled ginkgoes and garbage.

When Matthew came into the kitchen, she said, "I want to call the numbers."

"Can we just catch our breath?" He reached up across her and turned on the stove's fan, turned it up as far as it could go.

"I have them written down."

"Jesus Christ," he said over the fan's whirring. "We've had a streak of crazy. Or haven't you noticed? *Have* you noticed?"

She poured more water and drank it down. "Do you remember once when we called the numbers there was that girl—the roommate—who hesitated before saying no when we asked if she'd heard from Leda? It was like a millisecond but we both heard it. Remember?"

"I don't remember half of what you remember. You know this."

"I do."

Sometimes Sarah and Matthew blocked their own numbers, revealed their numbers; they each did the math and traveled through time zones, imagining where Leda might be. Sometimes they called all of them—one after the other.

She began riffling through the drawer below the phone, looking for the notebook.

"Just stop, Sarah." He sounded severe. "I need you to stop."

The bok choy, the fish, the pot of rice. The diced avocado in the small blue bowl.

She realized she was nodding, biting her lip so hard it hurt.

"Why can't you back off from it right now? Was it the mugging? I'm sorry you got hurt." He put his hands on both sides of her face. "I'm sorry."

"You are, I know you are. And I'm not sure what else I would have wanted you to do."

"But you are sure." He didn't let go of her face.

"What are you talking about?"

"You wanted me to beat him up."

"What?" She laughed. "That's insane."

"You wanted me to kill him."

She shrugged off his hands. "Of course I didn't want you to *kill him*."

He backed away from her but nodded calmly. "That's what you wanted. It's what you still want."

"No, I didn't."

"Yes, you did."

Her face flushed.

He stopped nodding.

"Fine," she said. "Fine, I did."

"Listen"—he leaned back on the counter—"you need to figure out what you're going to do."

"About what?"

"About you. About anything. Start with Caroline. You have an agent who still believes in you. She cared enough to make the suggestion."

"Are you kidding? That's what you think is most important right now?"

"You need to do something." It seemed as if he'd say more, but instead he opened the refrigerator. He took out a beer and twisted off the top, let it fall to the kitchen floor. "Sarah, she's not coming back. Maybe one day she will, but it won't be anytime soon."

Sarah picked up the bottle top from the floor and threw it across the kitchen.

"Jesus!" cried Matthew.

"No matter how many times you say this, I will never believe it. So you don't need to say it anymore. You can stop. You can stop saying she's not coming back. You can stop saying she's gone. Do you understand?"

"I heard from her."

"You—"

"I heard from her."

"But you swore—"

"Because I didn't think you could take it. I still don't think

196 JOANNA HERSHON

you can take it, but you know what? Neither can I. Because no matter what I do in the name of protecting you, it's always useless. So I guess I'm saying, screw it." He ran his hand over his face. "I heard from her."

"When."

"Two months ago. She said she was going to Mexico City with some people from the organization. She asked me not to tell you. She said she was building an internal civilization and having it manifest in the external world."

"You heard from her."

"Yes."

Sarah sliced a lime on the cutting board. She squeezed it over the diced avocado. Then she turned off the oven and the stove; she turned off the fan.

"Sarah—"

She grabbed her sweater from where she'd tossed it on the banister and walked back out into the night.

NOTHING ABOUT THE BAR, which was just a bar (*No food, old man, sorry*), was distinctive: Waylon Jennings on the stereo, twinkly lights, a tattered American flag. The bartender was presumably the old man's son; she'd seen him stacking the glassware, waving his father's smoke away. Sarah realized why she'd continued to watch him go about such a mundane task: he was attractive. She almost laughed out loud. The man's appeal hadn't struck her at first, but it seemed pretty obvious now.

She ordered a Manhattan, her voice sounding shrill and shaky.

He rubbed his eyes and squinted. "What was that? Can you speak up?" He didn't have a trace of an accent.

She repeated herself.

He nodded. "Got it. Sorry."

"No"—Sarah shrugged—"I'm a low talker."

"I'm just really beat." He poured bourbon into a shaker.

"Me too."

"Is that right? Rough day? You got a baby at home?"

"No," she said, hard.

"I don't know why I asked that. That's none of my business. This neighborhood just seems colonized by babies and their attractive parents."

"I'm a little old for that."

"Well, now you're just fishing." He looked at Sarah and she didn't look away. She willed herself not to flush at the base of her neck, where she could feel the blotches blooming. She was not half-naked; she was not acting impulsively. She was a grown woman sitting at a bar, making conversation.

"So, last night I cut off this guy when I realize how drunk he is. He gets belligerent. I tell him to go home, and he immediately passes out. I spend the rest of the night getting him to a hospital and answering questions."

"Sounds rough. But . . . he's okay?"

"Oh, he's fine." The bartender was evidently in no hurry to mix her drink. He balanced a cherry on a spoon, held on to it. "I mean, job hazard, I realize, but this is exactly the type of bullshit I was hoping to avoid when I opened a bar on the fringes of a bourgeois neighborhood. Not dealing with this bullshit is what I tell myself I'm getting in return for ponying up this kind of rent every month."

"And the attractive parents."

He dropped in the cherry, placed the glass on the bar. "Well, of course. That goes without saying."

She took a sip. It was cold and smoky, completely delicious. She wondered why she ever bothered with wine. "You know, bourgeois drunks are still drunk."

"Wise woman." He cracked his first real smile. "And you're neither."

"How can you tell?"

"No system. It's just a guess."

"Hmm, I don't know. I think the bruise on my face is making me more interesting."

"Wait. Wait, I recognize you."

Sarah felt a jolt of fear that he was a former classmate of Leda's. This was irrational because he had to be at least thirty-five. But maybe he'd been a teacher? A neighbor? "Probably from this bourgeois neighborhood?"

"Maybe." He seemed slightly deflated. "Probably."

"You must see a lot. Between people, I mean."

He shrugged. "I don't pay attention."

"Somehow I don't believe that's true."

"I drove a cab for a summer on Long Island. That was crazier."

"Yeah?"

"Oh yeah. Sure. People need to talk."

During the first of many pregnancies after Leda had turned

two, Sarah had been invited to speak at a film festival in Glasgow; on the way to JFK, she and the Sudanese taxi driver had spoken at length. He told her proudly that his wife was pregnant. He already had a toddler, a girl, who was exactly Leda's age. He revealed the due date, which was also Sarah's secret due date; the coincidence was too much, and so even though it was early and she'd not yet said it aloud to anyone besides Matthew, she told the driver that she was pregnant, too. They wished each other well; she miscarried on the flight home.

"What's the craziest thing you've heard?" Sarah asked now.

"It blends together. Y'know?"

"I do. I wish I didn't, but I do."

He placed both his hands on the bar. "I'm Alex." When he noticed her reaction, he smiled tightly. "What? What was that face for? Do you have a cute expression for every thought or something?"

"What did I do?" she blurted, and almost said, *I have a son named Alex. A beautiful imaginary son.*

"You have a very expressive face."

"I do not. In fact, I've always been told the opposite."

"Not sure what blind jackasses you've been talking to."

She was too flustered to say anything else.

"So . . . is Alex your husband's name or something?"

"No. No. My husband's name is Matthew."

"Aha. Okay."

The door opened and two couples came in, bringing with them a trace of moonlight. Beyond them was the same street she knew, a slice of inky sky. Cars and trucks took this corner too fast, and Sarah imagined being in one of those cars, driving out of the city, out of her life entirely. Leda's absence, she realized, was the center of her life. She'd chosen to make it so. She watched as the couples deliberated and Alex attentively offered them tastes of what was on draft, giving a lengthy description of a local IPA. He rolled up his sleeves with particular care; she expected some ink but there was none. By the time he made his way back to Sarah, she'd finished her drink. She smoothed bills down on the sticky wood.

"Going already?"

She nodded. "Did you ever serve food here?"

"Why? You hungry?"

She shook her head and looked over at the couples, laughing and touching each other's arms. "I met your father. That's why I came in here. He recommended it. I met him on the subway and he asked me for directions."

"You met my father on the subway?"

"I don't know why I didn't mention it right away." Alex's eyes were brown, his skin many shades darker than his father's. "He seemed like a nice man."

He nodded. "My father—"

"I was in a strange mood when he struck up a conversation"— she leaned forward—"but, actually, he seemed like more than a nice man. He seemed like a remarkable person, and—"

"My father has dementia," Alex said matter-of-factly. "He's not supposed to leave his house in Yonkers without the attendant. He shows up sometimes, but he doesn't remember. He thinks that I'm a world-class chef."

"Oh." Sarah could feel her lips pressing tightly together. For one brief moment, she had to close her eyes. "Oh."

Leda was gone. She knew this. *Stop making me say it*, Matthew yelled, the night she returned from Baja, his voice hoarse with tears. After a lifetime of shunning exercise, he started running the very next morning.

"That must be painful," she said.

"Of course it is. It's also a pain in the ass."

It was quiet between them and then it was silent.

"I'm Sarah." She couldn't meet his eyes.

Sometimes she thought she had nothing left: no more despair, no more desire. She was always wrong.

SARAH HAD BEEN BREATHLESS on that beach. Mainly from so much walking and the sun and wind, but also the phenomenal beauty. The sky was the same bright Pacific sky that loomed above her Pasadena rental, but it looked entirely different next to the jutting cliffs, next to the lush palm groves in the distance, so dense they looked black.

It's enough, Sarah had said.

She didn't know if Leda had heard her. Leda had hurled herself toward the sand and done five cartwheels after all. Then she lowered herself to the ground. She knelt for about a minute with her eyes closed. She did a slow and perfect headstand.

It's enough, Sarah had repeated, louder now. But Leda didn't come down. She was standing on her head and, from the looks of things, could have stayed that way for the rest of the afternoon.

It's time to come home.

Leda folded her legs into her body and slowly, effortlessly, sat upright again. *Please,* Sarah had said. *Just please.*

Please, what?

You think you're the only person who craves escape? Sarah cried. *Sweetie, you are not.*

Leda laughed.

Sarah sat down next to her in the warm sand. *You know what Spanish expression I love?* Sarah picked up the sand and let it run through her fingers. *Mi vida.* "My life." *People say it the way we say honey or sweetie. Pass the salt, my life. Call me when you get there, my life. It's so much more honest. English endearments are about sweetness, which is ridiculous. Because "my life" is what we really mean, at least with our children.*

I wasn't aware you spoke Spanish, Leda said bitingly.

You aren't sweet. And neither am I.

We're not the same.

I'm not saying we are. I'm saying you are my life.

You're saying we're the same. You think we are. And I can't believe you think it's some big secret that you crave escape.

I'll tell you anything you want to know. I'll always tell you anything.

But, Mom. Leda turned toward Sarah and, in one terrifying moment, stared her down. *I don't want it. I want to be separate.* Then Leda fixed her focus on the waves, which were closing out on the shoreline.

I'm staying here, Leda finally said.

These people. Leda, these people are unhinged.

These people are fine. I'm happy. I invited you here to tell you that. So you could let me go. You've got to let me go.

Never.

But Sarah had flown back to New York and returned to her life, which was the life of their family, which wasn't a family without their daughter. She was forty-eight years old. Leda was twenty-four.

FALL

I T WAS FOUR O'CLOCK IN THE MORNING. Summer was long gone. It had been an unseasonably warm fall. *Apocalyptic* was a word that often came up in conversation while merely discussing the weather. Winter was coming, and surely these habitual walks would stop, though for now, while unable to sleep, she hit the pavement. She was often out in the middle of the night. It was mid-November. She was not sleeping with Alex the bartender or anyone aside from her husband. What to send Sylvie for Christmas and Hanukkah? Should she send two separate presents? Matthew mentioned he'd sent another check to their new address in Jackson Heights, Queens. A casting director had hired Arman for a national gig. Kiki had texted a photo of Sylvie on Halloween, dressed up as a fox.

Sarah walked not toward the park but through the neighborhoods: down the hill, across the canal to the storage facility, where she considered visiting their unit. It was open 24-7. *So good to know*, she remembered joking with Matthew when they first rented the space. *Can there be a sadder time than the middle of the night to deal with one's possessions?* She imagined nodding to the receptionist, taking the elevator, walking the fluorescent-lit corridor. She could sit on the cold and dusty floor with the plastic tubs of stuffed animals and photos and irrelevant documents. She could cry over carefully folded baby clothes. Always an option. She could cry over the fact that she might never have grandchildren. Or that if she did have grandchildren, she wouldn't know them. But she kept walking all the way to the waterfront, to the pier with its scrabbly rocks that seemed to beckon a climb.

On her way there she'd walked quickly, barely noticing her surroundings, but on the way back, she took it slow. When she reached the canal, she stood on the bridge, alone under the scant moon and glaring streetlights, fearful of who might be out at this hour, but also marveling at how the stench from the polluted canal was absent. The air smelled so clean. On the other side of the bridge stood a lush patch of sunflowers. She always wondered who tended such an impressive garden, one that grew more elaborate each year, seemingly left alone to flourish. She thought, as she always did, how Leda had loved this bridge and this garden and how she—in a parallel universe or maybe even in this one—would enjoy being with Sarah there, right then. She thought of how they both loved small pockets of wonder, sought beauty in rough places. Leda had berated her for pointing out their similarities, but it had been so long, Sarah realized, since anyone else had done so. Then she crossed the bridge and looked more closely at the garden and—preposterously—saw a young junkie passed out in the sunflowers, streetlight shining brightly on her acne-scattered face. Dyed-green hair, nose pierced, cheek pierced, eyebrow pierced, and there Sarah was, seized with such revulsion that she turned away and ran onto the bridge, gripping the railing and dry heaving as she had done during all of her pregnancies, trying and failing for some kind of release into the foul water below.

Dear Caroline, I'm embarrassed it's taken me this long to thank you for our lunch.

When she walked up the hill and through the familiar pattern of streets, she realized dawn was breaking. She pictured the lake upstate and wondered when it would freeze. She still wondered what had happened to the woman who'd flopped around in the shallows. For a while she'd felt strangely guilty for not getting involved that day. It was as if, in her imagination, that woman had become Leda and Sarah had abdicated her clear responsibility to get her out of the water, that demeaning situation. But at some point Sarah had started telling herself another story. In this version, the woman at the lake was an excellent swimmer. She was faking it. She was playing him for reasons only she could understand.

Dear Caroline, I've been thinking it over.

Dear Caroline, You may be right.

Sarah took her phone from her back pocket.

Two months ago, the young man at the Apple store had plugged in her new phone. She'd seen all her contacts for Leda and immediately started weeping. The young man at the Apple store had kindly looked away. Then he'd asked for her credit card.

She didn't dial Leda's old numbers.

As she scrolled her phone's contacts, Sarah worried about waking her, even though she'd been assured many times that this was a good time to call.

"Hi," Kiki answered on the second ring.

"Good morning."

"You okay?"

Sarah looked around. Pearly sky, dull security grilles. "I am." She breathed in and smelled yeast from a bakery up the block. "What are you working on?"

"It's my fifth day on this new line. I'm using India ink. Lots of circles. I've been getting up every morning at four thirty."

"You're cuckoo for Cocoa Puffs."

"I know."

Sarah stood up straighter and looked across the street. A cheery neon sandwich blinked from a bodega window. "Is Sylvie still asleep?"

"She is," Kiki whispered.

Sarah smiled easily and felt a loosening in her chest. "Whatever you're doing is definitely working."

"You think? I don't know. It's working this week."

"What did you eat for breakfast?"

"Oh, it was so good." Kiki laughed. "You know that's what motivates me to get out of bed."

"I do."

"So I put leftover rice in a bowl with some spinach. I heated that, topped it with a fried egg and chopped avocado, sesame oil and soy sauce."

"Yum."

"Oh, and hot sauce."

"Tell me about the India ink."

"Oh, and toasted sesame seeds."

"Tell me about the circles."

MATTHEW WOULDN'T FALL back to sleep because once he was up, he was up. He'd make his way through the apartment and, when he failed to find Sarah, would find a scribbled note. He always would. She would never make him wonder. Then he'd suit up for his run, his sneakers hitting the pavement as she made her way home. Out and back, in and out, both of them moving through their life.

The anguish of death is different from the awareness of self-destruction.

You saw her alive on a beautiful beach just over a year ago.

There's hope is what he said.

There's time.

THEN THEY WENT for weeks without mentioning her.

Sarah bought Matthew an extravagant watch, not unlike the one that Arman had worn in the water. Matthew surprised Sarah with tickets to a show he knew she wanted to see. When the lights went down in the opulent theater, her pulse raced as if she were due onstage.

Dear Caroline, No, I haven't. I haven't been thinking it over. I'm not there. At least I'm not there yet.

As the lights went down, Matthew leaned over as if he were going to whisper to her, but he didn't. She put her hand on his thigh. Her gratitude became something else and she breathed in his ear, suddenly sick with desire. The set was a stark brick wall. The actors onstage looked lit from within. At first it seemed unintentional, as if one of the costumes hadn't been properly cleaned, but then it was unmistakable: sand—or, wait, ashes—spilled from all of the actors' sleeves each time anyone moved. The sand, the ashes, they also floated upward in the spotlights while simultaneously falling. When Sarah lay down at night, when she finally closed her eyes, it felt something like this. His thigh, her hand, awake, alive. In the theater, in their bed, she suddenly grabbed Matthew's hand. She often saw Leda's new teeth. She stroked Matthew's thigh; she clutched him. She left the house they shared. She came home. *Mi vida mi vida mi vida.* The teeth flashed like shells on the shoreline. They were breaking apart. They were coming together. They came and went with the tide.

Acknowledgments

This book was inspired by a short story I wrote called (confusingly) "Saint Ivo" and also by a conversation I had with my husband, Derek Buckner, who's an essential reader of everything I write. Derek, thank you for that conversation, your encouragement, and your truest support.

Jennifer Gilmore, Joanna Rakoff, Elisa Albert, Sallie Sills, Laura Rebell Gross, Catherine Lloyd Burns, and Merrill Feitell—huge thanks to all of you for reading that story and offering various forms of indispensable advice. I'm grateful to Dorian Karchmar and also Eve Attermann at WME. Thank you to *Granta*, especially to Rosalind Porter, for such an engaging editorial process, and to Sigrid Rausing for connecting with "Saint Ivo" and publishing it so thoughtfully.

Ellen Umansky read the first draft of this novel and gave me remarkable notes as always, as well as the faith to continue. Hilary Reyl and Jennifer Cody Epstein were both soulful and seriously smart readers. Hilary—thank you for that brilliant twist. Eliza Factor, Bliss Broyard, Sharon Guskin, and Nina Collins: I treasured those sustaining evenings, the individual and collective insights. Thank you, Lizzie Gottlieb, for an encouraging early read, Lauren and Ben Shenkman for many steps along the way, and Tanya Larkin—cherishing writerly friendship since 1989.

Thanks to Scott Adkins, Erin Courtney, and the Brooklyn Writers Space, where I've written three books during my time as a member. I highly recommend this quiet safe haven for writers.

Thank you, Julie Orringer, Nell Freudenberger, and everyone in that wise circle who offered advice and encouragement during the publication process.

My agent and dear friend for more than twenty years, Elizabeth Sheinkman at Peters, Fraser & Dunlop: you have my forever gratitude.

Jenna Johnson, my keen editor: all of our conversations are thought-provoking, and I'm very grateful for your brilliant work. Heartfelt thanks to Lydia Zoells, Brian Gittis, and everyone at Farrar, Straus and Giroux, where I am so fortunate to have landed with *St. Ivo*.

And, of course, I'm beyond grateful for my family—chaos, music, and boundless love.

A NOTE ABOUT THE AUTHOR

Joanna Hershon is the author of four novels: *Swimming, The Outside of August, The German Bride,* and *A Dual Inheritance.* Her writing has appeared in *Granta, The New York Times, One Story, Virginia Quarterly Review,* and two literary anthologies: *Brooklyn Was Mine* and *Freud's Blind Spot.* She teaches fiction in the MFA program at Columbia University and lives in Brooklyn with her husband, the painter Derek Buckner, and their three children.